Also by Paul Noth

How to Sell Your Family to the Aliens

HOW TO PROPERLY DISPOSE OF PLANET EARTH

PAUL NOTH

BLOOMSBURY
CHILDREN'S BOOKS

NEW YORK   LONDON   OXFORD   NEW DELHI   SYDNEY

BLOOMSBURY CHILDREN'S BOOKS
Bloomsbury Publishing Inc., part of Bloomsbury Publishing Plc
1385 Broadway, New York, NY 10018

BLOOMSBURY, BLOOMSBURY CHILDREN'S BOOKS, and the Diana logo
are trademarks of Bloomsbury Publishing Plc

First published in the United States of America in January 2019
by Bloomsbury Children's Books

Bloomsbury books may be purchased for business or promotional use. For information on bulk
purchases please contact Macmillan Corporate and Premium Sales Department at
specialmarkets@macmillan.com

Library of Congress Cataloging-in-Publication Data
Names: Noth, Paul, author, illustrator.
Title: How to properly dispose of Planet Earth / by Paul Noth.
Description: New York : Bloomsbury, 2019. | Sequel to: How to sell your family to the aliens.
Summary: With Squeep's help, Hap Conklin, eleven, faces his fear of talking to the
new girl at school but also opens a black hole and uncovers information
about his grandmother's next evil plan.
Identifiers: LCCN 2018024639 (print) | LCCN 2018030283 (e-book)
ISBN 978-1-68119-659-6 (hardcover) • ISBN 978-1-68119-660-2 (e-book)
Subjects: | CYAC: Middle schools—Fiction. | Schools—Fiction. | Family Life—Fiction. |
Lizards as pets—Fiction. | Grandmothers—Fiction. | Science fiction. | Humorous stories.
Classification: LCC PZ7.1.N66 Hop 2019 (print) | LCC PZ7.1.N66 (e-book) |
DDC [Fic]—dc23
LC record available at https://lccn.loc.gov/2018024639

Book design by Jeanette Levy
Typeset by Westchester Publishing Services
Printed and bound in the U.S.A. by Berryville Graphics Inc., Berryville, Virginia
2 4 6 8 10 9 7 5 3 1

All papers used by Bloomsbury Publishing Plc are natural, recyclable products made from wood
grown in well-managed forests. The manufacturing processes conform to the environmental
regulations of the country of origin.

To find out more about our authors and books visit www.bloomsbury.com and
sign up for our newsletters.

For my parents,
Louise and Dominique Paul Noth

PART 1

"SURRENDER, HAPPY!"

CHAPTER 1

THE POSSIBILITIES

I, Happy Conklin Jr., am now eleven. Over the past year
I've learned a lot about what's possible and what's not . . .

SELLING MY WHOLE FAMILY TO THE ALIENS, WHEN
I ONLY MEANT TO SELL MY GRANDMA . . .

POSSIBLE!

TRAVELING ACROSS THE UNIVERSE
VIA A BLACK HOLE IN MY SISTER
ALICE'S MAKEUP COMPACT . . .

POSSIBLE!

FLAMENCO DANCING WITH MY GRANDMA IN AN ALIEN DEATH MATCH . . .

POSSIBLE!

ASKING NEVADA EVERLY TO BE MY LAB PARTNER . . .

NOT POSSIBLE!

Why was asking Nev Everly to be my lab partner so impossible? Because my mouth refused to talk to her and my brain turned to useless goulash in her presence.

I didn't realize Nev's effect on me the first time I saw her. I only noticed that a smiling girl with long brown hair stood in front of our homeroom. Her vintage clothes made it seem like she had wandered in out of an old Hollywood movie.

"Class," said Ms. York. "We have a new student. Nevada, would you like to introduce yourself to the class?"

"Not really," said Nev.

I laughed.

I overheard her say two more things that made me laugh in our first-hour science class.

She's funny, I thought. *You're funny too. You should ask her to be your lab partner.*

So I walked up to her to introduce myself.

Then I walked past her.

I ended up in the back of the room sharpening a pencil.

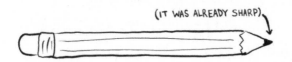

(IT WAS ALREADY SHARP)

At lunch that day, I stood in line behind a talkative kid named Felix, who for some reason always called me by my last name, Conklin.

"Actually, Conklin . . . ," Felix was saying.

Nev Everly got into the lunch line right behind me.

"Hi!" said Felix. "You're actually the new girl! I'm Felix."

"Hey," she said. "I'm Nev."

"So, actually . . . ," said Felix, "do you want me to show you around the cafeteria?"

"I've been in a cafeteria before," said Nev.

I pretended not to know Felix.

"This is my buddy Conklin," he said, putting his arm around me.

"Hi," said Nev.

That's when my brain melted into goulash.

I said nothing. I only stared at her.

"Conklin and I both have lizards," said Felix.

"Huh," said Nev.

"It's actually true," said Felix, looking at me. "You know, come to think of it, Conklin, since we both have lizards, we should be lab partners in science class. We could actually do a lizard science project! How awesome would that be?"

As Felix worked himself into a lather about all the reptile experiments we could do together, I fought back the urge to knock him on the head with my lunch tray.

CHAPTER 2

ACTUALLY . . .

Felix had attached himself to me on the first day of sixth grade. He seemed to want to be my best friend but also to correct every word that came out of my mouth.

"Actually, Conklin," he'd say, "it's pronounced 'orangu-TAN,' not 'orangu-TANG.'"

hang in there

"Actually, Conklin," he'd say seconds later. "Chimpanzees aren't monkeys, they're great apes."

"Actually, Conklin . . . Actually, Conklin . . . Actually, Conklin . . ."

I don't mind being corrected when I'm wrong, but Felix racked up at least fifty *Actually, Conklins* on any given school day.

And after the first twenty, you start to feel like an idiot.

Felix also tended to speak at great length about his favorite subject, the digestive troubles of his pet lizard, the Mighty Thor.

After a few months of this, I made the mistake of telling him that I, too, had a pet lizard, by the name of Squeep!

"*Actually*, Conklin?" said Felix. "We both have lizards? Get out. What are the friggin' odds?"

Why had I ever mentioned Squeep! or called him my "pet lizard"?

That wasn't accurate.

Squeep! was nobody's pet, and he hadn't been a proper lizard ever since Alice stole him and stashed

him in the Doorganizer, an infinite closet powered by a black hole.

This journey through extra-dimensional space-time had altered Squeep! in profound and disturbing ways.

Sure, he still looked like a lizard, but he acted more like an ambassador from another dimension. He seemed to have diplomatic immunity to our laws of physics. He'd escape from wherever I put him and show up wherever I least expected, sometimes only seconds later.

He'd moved out of his terrarium at my old elementary school, which was understandable. Once you've lived in a black hole and crisscrossed the galaxy, who could go back to sitting on a rock and eating bugs all day? Besides, a new lizard named Pete had replaced him as the class pet. So Squeep! decided to move in with me. Most mornings I awoke to find him sleeping on my forehead or chest.

He wasn't so much a "pet" as a "scaly roommate who slept on my head."

I preferred Squeep! to any normal pet.

Normal pet lizards need to be fed, cared for, and cleaned up after. They're also—if you believe Felix—prone to constipation. The Mighty Thor could only poop in a warm-water bath. Felix said his family was always arguing about whose turn it was to "poop the lizard."

Thankfully, Squeep! preferred finding his own food, and I never had to worry about how he went to the bathroom, except when I accidentally walked in on him.

But I didn't like Squeep!'s constant disappearing and reappearing. I called it his Lizardini routine, after the famous escape artist Harry Lizardini.

It unnerved me whenever he pulled a Lizardini, but especially the time I discovered him inside my school locker. He sat in the upper compartment, staring at me. He refused to come out.

After some coaxing, I tried closing the locker door, just to show him I meant business. But when I reopened it a moment later, Squeep!

had vanished, leaving behind a single gray seashell. I spent the rest of the day scratching my head about how and why he had done that.

I began noticing other little "parting gifts" that Squeep! would leave for me whenever he disappeared: the seashell, a nacho chip, a bottle cap.

It felt like he was trying to tell me something with these little doodads.

But what?

I even started a "Doodad Decoder" in the back of my pre-algebra notebook to figure out what each one meant.

Doodad Decoder

SEASHELL $= X$

NACHO $= Y$

BOTTLE CAP $= Z$

CHAPTER 3

ALICE'S BROTHER

Before Nev showed up, my confidence at school had improved a lot, ever since the incident with the aliens last year.

After surviving that traumatic ordeal, getting teased by fifth graders no longer bothered me. It took more than being called "Beard Boy" to hurt my feelings.

When I stopped crying, the Make-Beard-Boy-Cry Dance seemed kind of pointless to everyone.

I even started getting along with some of the other kids, though not Willow Johansen. She never forgave me for ruining the dance she invented.

But still, I had reason to hope that Wonder Street Middle School would be a fresh start.

Then, on my first day of sixth grade, some seventh-grade boy started picking on me in the hallway.

"Hey, Dinky!" he yelled, walking toward me. His

friend, who looked frightened, grabbed him by the shoulder and said two words:

"Alice's brother."

The kid who'd called me Dinky froze. The color fell from his face.

"Sorry," he croaked.

They both backed away as though I were a stray pit bull foaming at the mouth.

Wherever I went that morning, a whispered "Alice's brother" echoed among the big kids as they took frightened, furtive glances at me.

That afternoon, I couldn't find the gym, so I walked up to this giant kid to ask for directions. He must have been an eighth grader because that's as high as the school went, though he looked about nineteen. He wore a varsity football jersey. Number 07.

"Excuse me," I said.

Glancing down at me, his eyes popped open like he'd been electrically shocked.

He took a wallet out of his pocket and threw it at me.

"Just take it!" he screamed, and ran away.

I chased after him to give him his wallet back, which

only scared him more. Looking back in horror, he took off like a rhino and left me in the dust.

Not knowing what else to do, I carried his wallet to the school office and told them that I had found it on the floor. The secretaries and an assistant principal began close-talking and sneaking looks at me. I heard the same echoing whisper:

"Alice's brother . . . that's Alice's brother."

Adults too? How could grown-ups be afraid of Alice, an eighth-grade girl? I asked my little sister Kayla—who knows everything—about it after school.

"I don't get it," I said. "Alice hasn't had the Doorganizer for months, but everyone still acts like she's all-powerful."

"She still has her reputation," said Kayla.

"But what are the adults so afraid of?" I asked.

"Blackmail," said Kayla.

"Blackmail?" I said. "Who's Alice blackmailing?"

"Whoever she has to," said Kayla. "How do you think she got away with thieving for so long? By stealing information too. She's got everyone's secrets in her head, to use as *kompromat*. She knows things about Principal Kellogg that would curl your hair."

I didn't believe it until I saw it with my own eyes.

Alice would come and go from school, right in front of the security guards, whenever she pleased. I once saw her walk out of the teacher's lounge drinking a soda she had gotten from their vending machine!

As "Alice's brother," I found that I could get away with things too. I tried not to take advantage of this, but sometimes it was irresistible. Like if I saw an older kid picking on a fellow sixth grader, I could be a big hero just by strolling up and saying, "Is there a problem here?"

The bully would squeak an apology and flee, leaving my fellow sixth graders baffled. Most of them had known me since kindergarten. No one had *ever* been afraid of Happy Conklin Jr.

What had changed over the summer?

Someone started the rumor that I'd become a karate master.

Okay, I started that rumor. I'm not proud of it.

No sooner had I started enjoying my new charmed life than something happened to burst my bubble. Mr. Jamneky, a math teacher new to the school, gave me a C in pre-algebra. My dad freaked out.

When Dad was my age he was doing advanced calculus, so he expected far greater things from me than Cs in pre-algebra.

I guess I should have spent more time in class taking

notes and less time working on the Doodad Decoder in the back of my notebook.

But the doodads were so much more interesting.

Squeep! had continued to leave them behind whenever he disappeared. In addition to the seashell, the nacho chip, and the bottle cap, he now sometimes left a quarter and a chocolate Easter egg. These last two always appeared together.

What on earth did *that* mean?

Then came the silver snake ring.

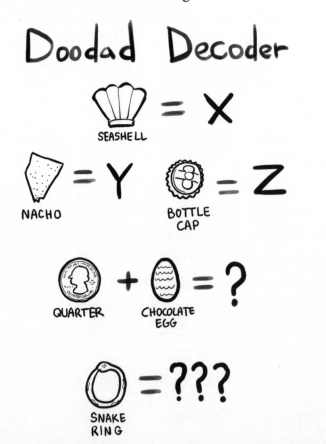

Doodad Decoder

SEASHELL = X

NACHO = Y   BOTTLE CAP = Z

QUARTER + CHOCOLATE EGG = ?

SNAKE RING = ???

CHAPTER 4

THE SILVER SNAKE RING

Squeep! and I lounged on the living room carpet, half listening to my sister Beth as she taught Baby Lu about Genghis Khan.

Baby Lu loved being read to so much that she would sit still for almost anything. This allowed Beth to babysit while also studying for her ninth-grade Civilizations exam.

"Genghis Khan," read Beth, "and his Mongolian horde of mounted archers swept through Asia, slaughtering over one-tenth of the

people on Earth and conquering nearly one-quarter of the land. His was the most violent reign in all human history . . ."

Baby Lu looked fascinated.

When I turned back to Squeep!, he had vanished.

In his place on the carpet gleamed a silver ring. I picked it up and brought it to the window for a better look.

Its heaviness on my palm gave me a spooky yet familiar feeling.

I knew this ring from somewhere.

The silver had been forged into the shape of a snake biting its own tail. Its red gemstone eyes so captivated my attention that I failed to notice the approach of Eliza, Beth's twin sister.

"Whoa!" said Eliza, snatching the ring from my hand. "This is Grandma's! Where did you find Grandma's ring?"

"It was right here on the carpet," I said truthfully, though I didn't say anything about Squeep!

"It's the *Ouroboros*," said Eliza. "The symbol of eternal return. Maybe it means . . . Grandma's coming back."

Her mouth fell open into a smile as her eyes glimmered down at the circular serpent.

"Yeah," she said. "It must mean Grandma's coming back. What else *could* it mean? Beth, Grandma's coming back!"

Beth gave me a worried look.

We didn't share Eliza's enthusiasm for Grandma.

If you read my last book, you'll know why Grandma wasn't our favorite person.

She wasn't the FBI's favorite person either. She'd been at the top of their Ten Most Wanted Fugitives list for a year now. We still had federal agents in black SUVs staking out our apartment in case she returned.

She was, however, Eliza's favorite person. Because Eliza actually believed her ridiculous promises. See, Grandma had this lunatic plan to take over the galaxy. She said that if we helped her we would each be given our own solar system to rule over as queens and kings.

Insane? Absolutely. But Eliza believed every word of it. She spent idle hours daydreaming about her future kingdom.

"We've got to get ready," said Eliza breathlessly. "We've got to be ready for her return. Grandma's coming back!"

"If Grandma ever does come

back," I said, "they'll lock her up for breaking every law in the book."

"*When* Grandma comes back," said Eliza, fitting the ring onto her own finger, "she will be the only law."

These words sent a shiver down me timbers. Grandma was scary! I dreaded her return. And I hated the idea of her having anything to do with Squeep!'s disappearances and the weird doodads he left behind.

CHAPTER 5

LIZARDINI

Squeep! stayed disappeared for a few days, until I awoke one morning to find him sleeping on my head.

Felix had been pestering me about getting started on our science project, so I decided to act right away, before Squeep! vanished again.

I built a lizard carrier out of an old bowling ball bag and some mesh material, so Squeep! could breathe. I zipped him inside and carried him the three and a half blocks to Felix's house to meet the Mighty Thor.

"Actually, Conklin," said Felix, greeting me at his front door, "I was starting to wonder about you."

"Hey, Felix," I said.

I followed him up the stairs and into his bedroom, where the Mighty Thor sat looking bloated in a glass terrarium.

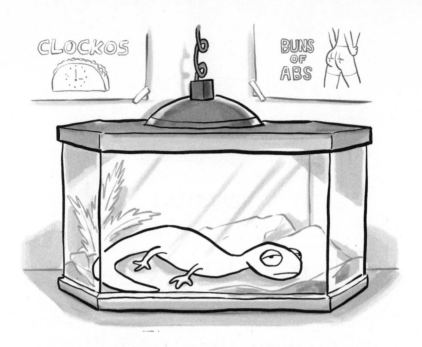

To my surprise, Felix had pictures of my dad, Hap Conklin Sr., on his wall. He had taped up articles about Dad's scientific breakthroughs and advertisements for his old inventions like Hap Conklin's Buns of Abs, and Clockos, "the only frozen taco that tells the time."

"Well, Conklin," said Felix. "Can I actually meet Squeep! now?"

I opened my lizard carrier to take him out, but all I found inside was a small gray seashell.

"What's that?" said Felix.

"Uh . . . a shell," I said.

"I can see that it's a shell," said Felix. "Where's your lizard?"

"He escaped," I said.

"Sure he escaped," said Felix, shaking his head.

"He must have," I said.

"Be honest, Conklin," said Felix. "You don't actually have a lizard, do you?"

"Why would I lie about having a lizard?"

"To impress me," said Felix. "I tell you about my lizard. You want to be cool too, so you say, 'Oh, I have a lizard!' when all you actually have is a seashell in a bowling ball bag."

"But I do really have a lizard," I said.

He gave me a pitying look.

"Sorry, Conklin," he said. "But I can't actually be your lab partner."

"What? How come?"

"I only asked you because I thought you might actually be smart, like your dad, which you're clearly not."

This was the wrong thing to say to me.

"Hey!" I said. "I do too have a lizard, and guess what, he's not constipated like yours. He's magic!"

"Ho," said Felix. "So now it's a magic lizard? Ho-ho!"

"Oh . . . go poop the Mighty Thor!" I said.

I stormed down the stairs and out the front door.

I fumed the whole walk home, until I remembered something:

I had never wanted to be Felix's lab partner in the first

place. I wanted to be Nev Everly's lab partner. And tomorrow I would ask her. This was just the push I needed. Tomorrow morning, first thing in homeroom, I would ask Nev to be my lab partner.

Well, I wouldn't just *ask* her . . . because that was impossible.

So I devised a clever plan that would make asking her *not* impossible.

First, I'd need a little help from my younger sister Kayla.

Then I would be able to ask Nev tomorrow.

And once we were lab partners . . . who knows?

Maybe we'd become math buddies.

CHAPTER 6

NEVER EVERLY

Nev's first name was Nevada, but I had started thinking of it as "Never," because talking to her seemed so impossible.

I figured my only hope was to make her laugh. That would break the ice between us, and then asking her to be my lab partner would stop being impossible. But I couldn't just walk up to her with some preplanned joke. That would look desperate. It needed to be spontaneous. The best way would be to wait until she made *me* laugh, and then hit her with a hilarious comeback. Here's how I saw it happening:

But here's what always happened instead:

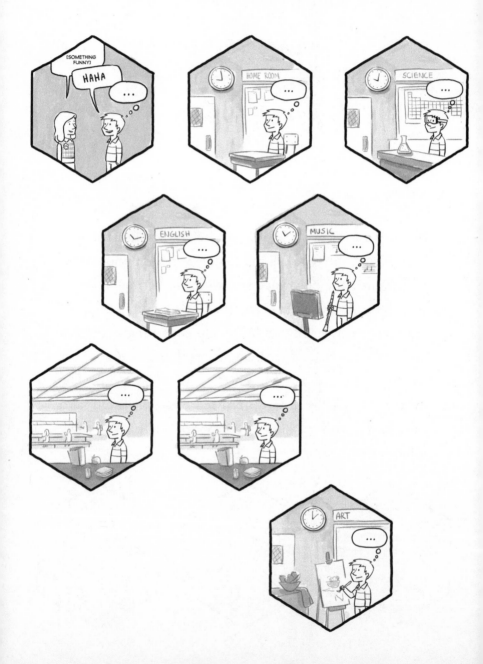

The perfect funny comeback always arrived way too late. What would have been genius at 11:00 a.m. was useless at 5:30 p.m.

And that's where my sister Kayla could be of help.

Kayla, now ten, had an imaginary bee named Alphonso who helped her predict the future. It sounds crazy, but if you've met Kayla, or read the last book, you know it really works.

Kayla could "attach" to anything she saw or heard.

So if she "attached" to me, she would see all my possible pasts and possible futures laid out in hexagons, like this:

In this honeycomb of time, Alphonso the bee was the

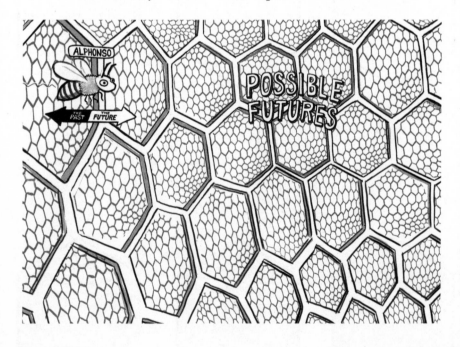

present moment. He was also Kayla's friend. She could ask Alphonso which of the trillions of possible pathways he was going to take, which of my possible futures would become my actual future, and he would tell her.

The only blind spot to Kayla's ability had been the Doorganizer. When something went into Alice's makeup compact, Kayla lost the trail and could no longer make predictions about it.

I didn't need her to see into a black hole, but only into my day tomorrow. Then she could tell me the funny thing Nev would say in class, and I would have hours to craft the most hilarious response possible.

This brilliant plan had only one snag. Kayla had stopped predicting things that would happen on Earth. These days she only wanted to attach to things she saw in the night sky through her telescope.

She believed astronomical predictions to be more important. Also, she could see a lot farther into the future up there. On Earth, life's endlessly complex interactions limited her range. It took hours of intense concentration for her to see into next week on Earth. But a spot of space through the telescope was so much less eventful she could see hundreds or even thousands of years ahead in minutes.

Every night she'd concentrate on a different tiny section of the sky and hunt for future asteroids of the sort that had wiped out the dinosaurs millions of years ago.

Once she got going on this, she wouldn't stop until our parents made her go to bed.

But I knew how to get her to take a break from her telescope. I brought her a bottle of her favorite soda, Tamarindo.

I found her in her usual evening spot on the roof of our building, sitting on a lawn chair beside the tripod of her plastic telescope and making little marks in a grid paper notebook.

CHAPTER 7

ASTEROIDINI

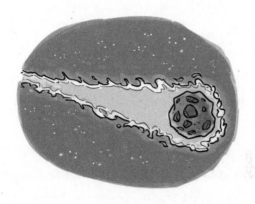

"**H**ow's it coming?" I asked.

"It's the weirdest thing," she said, without looking up. "A while ago I was tracking an asteroid about five hundred years in the future. But now I can't find it anymore. It's . . . just gone."

"Well, that's good, right?" I said. "If it's not there, it can't hit us."

"It's not good. Asteroids aren't supposed to disappear for no reason."

"Maybe you just need a break from that,"
I said. "Here, I brought you a Tamarindo."

"Oh," she said, perking up. "Thanks."

She took the bottle from me eagerly
but then paused before twisting off the
cap.

"Wait, you must want something from
me," she said. "I'm not going to predict
anything on Earth for you. I don't do
that anymore."

"You just did," I said. "You predicted I
wanted you to predict something."

"Well, that was obvious," she said, handing me back
the bottle. "Sorry, Hap, but no thanks."

"You can keep the soda if you listen to my idea. You
don't have to say yes. The soda's just for hearing me out."

"Fine," she said, twisting open the bottle. She took a
sip and smiled with deep satisfaction. Kayla loved all sweet
liquids. Maybe she was part honeybee herself. But her
smile faded as I told her my plan for getting Nev to be my
lab partner. By the time I finished she was shaking her
head at me.

"Come on," I said. "Why not?"

"Do I really need to tell you?" she said, turning back to
the eyepiece of her telescope.

"Aw, come on," I said. "It will take you three minutes."

"No," she said. "And that's final."

But I went on pestering her about it, until she got angry.

"Hap, I'm witnessing a serious astronomical paradox here," she yelled. "I'm not going to take a break to help you think of pickup lines."

Now this made *me* angry. That's not what I wanted her to do at all.

"Pickup lines?" I said, feeling my face flush. "That's not . . . I'm not trying to . . . Look, this is for science. I want her to be my lab partner in *science* class. By not helping, you're standing in the way of science."

She rolled her eyes in a way that infuriated me.

"You think you're so smart," I said. "But you don't know *anything* about people. All you care about is research and experiments. You're turning into Dad."

She shot me a look so angry that I took a step backward, because I knew she was about to juke me.

She didn't have to do that.

Yes, I had said something deliberately mean to hurt her feelings, but still . . . she didn't have to juke me for it.

Kayla discovered the juke a few months ago, while watching a soccer game on TV. That had been a dark day in the lives of her older siblings.

She had noticed how one player could use footwork and body language to throw the opposing player off balance or send him in the wrong direction. A useful trick in a soccer game became a deadly weapon in the hands of Kayla, who could predict a person's involuntary reactions to millions of possible moves before she made them.

Now on the roof, after I said, "You're turning into Dad," she leaped up like a cat, took two crazy steps toward me, and I fell over.

Still two feet away, she hadn't touched me. But she'd executed three perfect moves to make me trip over my own feet.

I landed painfully on the roof gravel. Springing back up, I ran away from Kayla as fast as I could toward the door. I knew better than to be around her when she was like this. But I couldn't resist the urge to turn and yell back the meanest thing I could think of, based on her greatest fear.

"I hope the FBI locks you up in a research hospital!" I yelled, noticing that she was about to throw the soda bottle at me.

She never actually threw it. This was another juke, designed to distract me so I would run straight into the side of the door.

Now I had a headache and lot of homework.

I would need to think of a science project I could do by myself, without Nev or Felix. Plus I had a lot of catch-up work in pre-algebra.

In my room, I dragged my backpack onto my bed to get started.

As I unzipped it, something dark moved inside.

It sprang out at me.

Leaping back, my hand clutched to my heart, I stared down at Squeep! the lizard.

"You!" I yelled. "What are you, trying to kill me?"

Squeep! stared up at me blankly. Lately his !-shaped body had been looking a lot more like a ? instead.

I squatted down to get some answers.

"Where do you keep disappearing to all the time?" I said.

He flicked his tail to his face and handed me a gray seashell.

"What's this supposed to mean?" I said, throwing it on the floor.

He flicked his tail to his face again and handed me the same seashell.

I threw it on the floor.

"Why do you keep giving me stuff?"

He flicked his tail and handed me a third identical gray shell.

He had pulled it out of thin air. Looking around, I couldn't find any of the shells I'd thrown on the floor. I examined the one in my hand.

A small gray shell. The shape of it reminded me of something. So did the idea of objects appearing out of nowhere . . .

"The makeup compact," I said. "Alice's makeup compact was shaped like this kind of shell."

Squeep! bobbed his head in a way eerily similar to a nod.

"That's what you've been trying to tell me, isn't it? Something about the Doorganizer? . . . They destroyed that thing. Last year."

Squeep! shook his head, a clear no.

Uh-oh.

"Is that where you keep going? Into the Doorganizer?" I held up the seashell. "Is this it? The shell. Is this the new portal?"

He shook his head.

"Where is it?" I asked.

He flicked his tail and handed me a nacho.

"It's in a nacho?"

He flicked his tail and handed me a poker chip with a picture of Elvis Presley on it.

This was insane. Where was he getting all this stuff from?

The Doorganizer, of course. It was all stuff Alice had stolen over the years. He was slipping in and out of time, grabbing things and slipping back seamlessly, just like she used to.

Not good, I thought. The Doorganizer was dangerous.

I knew I had to tell Dad, but I also knew that Alice must never find out.

After a year of therapy, Alice had made a bit of progress recovering from her obsessive manias. But this news could send her back off the deep end.

I decided to wait until Alice fell asleep, then tell Dad.

In the meantime, I tried to catch up on my pre-algebra. But I couldn't concentrate. Eventually, I turned to the Doodad Decoder in the back of my notebook.

Unfortunately, I wasn't any better at doodad algebra than I was at the regular kind.

Doodad Decoder

SEASHELL = Doorganizer

NACHO = X

QUARTER + **CHOCOLATE EGG** = Y

BOTTLE CAP = Z

POKER CHIP = ?

SNAKE RING = ???

CHAPTER 8

THE FRUIT FLY

Around midnight, I carried Squeep! into the hallway. The only light came from the crack under the door of Beth and Eliza's room. Alice and Kayla's threshold was dark. As I crossed the living room, I heard my parents having a hushed argument in the kitchen.

Dad stood painting a bowling ball with an experimental new varnish under the stove's vent fan.

As part of the parole deal that kept him out of prison, Dad had agreed to take a break from inventing and scientific research for a few years. He had taken the least scientific job he could find: day manager at Striker's Island bowling alley.

But quitting science proved impossible for someone like him. He became obsessed with improving the bowling equipment, until we had half-dissected balls, pins, bags, and shoes all over our apartment.

I stood unnoticed for a while at the edge of the kitchen.

"*You* tell Kayla come down the roof!" said Mom. Her English got worse when she was angry. "She not listen. Always on the telescope."

"Maybe she's discovered something," said Dad, dabbing his brush.

"It's twelve o'clock on the school night!" said Mom.

"Okay," said Dad. "Just give me a second to finish this."

"What Kayla say! Always 'give me second,' 'give me second.' You and her the same . . ." Mom said a Romanian word for a specific kind of crazy person. Then, noticing me standing there, she added, "Now this one up too. Nobody goes asleep."

"Hap, go to bed," said Dad.

"There's something wrong with Squeep!" I said, holding up the lizard as I walked in. "I think it might be serious."

"Uh-oh," said Dad. "Is he sick?"

"No, it's . . . weirder than that. Where do I start? . . . First, he can understand English."

Dad sighed and then shook his head, chuckling.

"Oh, Hap," he said. "Look, sometimes it seems like animals understand us. But really they're just reacting to our body language, or even reading our pheromones. You know, there was an interesting study in the *Journal of*—"

"Okay, okay," I said, trying to head off a dissertation before he got one going. "Here's what's really worrying me. Squeep! is still going in and out of"—I lowered my voice to a whisper—"the *Doorganizer*."

Dad's eyes popped open. Mom looked up in alarm.

"That's impossible," said Dad. "It no longer exists. I personally oversaw the demolition."

"Well, it's still there somehow," I said.

"We destroy the makeup compacts," said Mom. "They all gone."

"Tell that to Squeep!" I said. "Because he's still popping in and out of it every chance he gets. And bringing things back!"

"He can't be," said Dad. "There's nothing to pop in and out of. It's gone. There's no more micro black hole. No more portals."

"I think . . . maybe he *is* a portal," I said.

"A living organism can't be a portal," said Dad. "That's impossible for so many reasons. And even if it weren't . . .

even if a lizard somehow *could* be a portal, he could not then enter the Doorganizer through himself."

"Why not?" I said. "Isn't extra-dimensional space-time really weird like that?"

"It's really weird, but not like that," said Dad. "Look, you saw some strange things inside the Doorganizer, I know. But that doesn't mean you understand extra-dimensional space-time. It's a highly complex mathematical concept that, frankly, someone who gets Cs in pre-algebra—"

"I got *one* C."

"—is not equipped to comprehend. Sorry, Hap, but you just don't have the math to get this."

"Well," I said, a little annoyed now. "Really *good* scientists can put things in layman's terms, like with analogies and stuff. So that normal people can understand extra-dimensional space-time too."

"Analogies, huh?" said Dad, thinking. He pointed to the open window. "Okay, this window is a portal to the outside of our apartment. Imagine a fruit fly enters in through it, picks up this bowling ball, carries it all the way to the bowling alley, and then throws a perfect strike. *That's* more likely than you understanding extra-dimensional space-time."

"Hey!" said Mom. "That's not . . . *incurajator*."

"That means 'encouraging,'" I said to Dad. "See, I

actually learned Romanian, unlike you. Do you know what 'encouraging' means in English?"

"You're good with language, Hap," said Dad. "But you need to take math more seriously."

"But that's not how Happy learns," said Mom. "He's special."

"Mom, please don't call me that!" I said. "Guys, would you just trust me on something for once? Squeep! is seriously going into the Doorganizer."

"What!" said a voice from behind me. "The lizard's going into my closet?"

Wheeling around, I saw Alice standing in her nightgown at the threshold of the kitchen with an empty water glass.

"Of course not, sweetie," said Dad. "See what you started, Hap? The Doorganizer doesn't exist anymore. We destroyed all the compacts. Squeep!'s just been a little agitated lately. Maybe he's sick. Here, why don't I examine him."

Hearing this, Squeep! leaped out of my hands and scuttled across the kitchen floor.

Alice dropped down like a hockey goalie to catch Squeep!, who accelerated and zipped past her fingers.

"I told you he understands English!" I said.

Alice turned, stumbling to her feet and chasing him through the living room. I sprinted out of the kitchen to catch her before she caught him.

Around the next corner, in the hallway, I found her staring down at the place on the floor where Squeep! had vanished.

He had left something behind.

Alice bent down and lifted up . . . a green kazoo.

"This is mine," she said, glaring at me. "This is *my* kazoo."

"You mean it's a kazoo you stole once," I said.

"He's really going into my closet, isn't he?" said Alice. She slowly smiled. "It's still there. It's *all* still there . . . How's he doing it?"

"I don't know. That's what I was asking Dad."

"Bring me the lizard," said Alice. "When you find him, bring him straight to me."

"Why should I?"

"Because," she said, leaning in close. "I can make things good for you at school . . . or I can make things *really bad*."

"I know," I said.

"Good," said Alice. "So bring me the lizard."

She stalked off, clutching the green kazoo in her fist.

CHAPTER 9

THE BECKONING FLIPPER

After staying up so late, I slept through my alarm the next morning.

I didn't wake until Squeep! yanked my eyelids open.

"Gah!" I yelled, swatting him away. "What the heck, man!"

I blink-blink-blinked until my eyes stopped burning. Squeep! crouched on my bedspread staring up at me.

"Hey listen," I said. "Alice is after you. That's not good. You need to lie low, buddy, until the heat's off."

He flicked his tail to his face and handed me a seashell from out of nowhere.

"What! How do you keep doing that?" I said.

He did it again, but this time he moved so slowly that I could see the whole process, his tail curling around in slow motion until he looked like a question mark, and then farther, until his body formed a perfect circle. As the tip of his tail came to his face, his mouth bit down on it.

He vanished.

I said, "*Whaaaaat?*"

He reappeared, still in the perfect circular shape but holding a seashell. I shuddered, realizing how much he now looked like Grandma's ring, the snake biting its own tail. What had Eliza called it?

The Ouroboros, symbol of the eternal return.

Dropping the shell, Squeep! stayed circular with his mouth open over his tail-tip, ready to bite down again and vanish into the Doorganizer.

Then, looking up at me, he reached his flipper toward my hand, as though he wanted to pull me in there with him.

"No way!" I said, yanking my hand out of reach. "I'm not going back in *there*. Not ever again."

He beckoned me with his flipper.

"Come on," he seemed to be saying. "Time to go."

My heart pounded. It felt as if I were standing at the edge of the highest high dive in the world—a tiny voice in my mind saying, *Jump!*

"No, that's not gonna happen," I said, laughing nervously. "That place is the worst."

Come on, said my tiny inner voice. *It will make a great science project.*

I pictured how the triptych would look at the science fair:

I laughed, imagining Felix's reaction.

Dad would be pretty astonished too. He hated to be proved wrong. But I remembered my last trip into the Doorganizer all too well. I never wanted to experience that again.

"For the last time, no!" I said to Squeep!

Mom knocked on the door and yelled, "Happy! You're late!"

I jumped out of bed and began pulling on my school clothes. Then I ran to the bathroom and brushed my teeth. I didn't have time to shave, but I always carried a portable razor and shaving cream in my backpack. So I could take care of that in the school bathroom before class.

I jogged back into the bedroom to grab my backpack. It felt heavier than usual. Looking inside, I saw why. I had a reptilian stowaway.

Squeep!, curled in a perfect Ouroboros circle atop textbooks, held out his flipper.

"Get out of there!" I said. "I can't take you to school."

He wouldn't budge. I dared not reach in and grab him either, out of fear he would pull me into the Doorganizer.

With Alice after him, maybe he'd be safer with me today. I zipped it almost closed but left a little opening so he could breathe.

I ran from my room to the kitchen, where Mom stood, Baby Lu in one arm, the other holding out a piece of grape-jellied toast for me.

"Everybody waiting for you outside," she said.

"Sorry," I said, munching into the toast. "Bye, guys!"

I hurried down our apartment building's steps. Mom liked us all to walk together in the morning. We went to three different schools—Acorn Lane Elementary, Wonder Street Middle, and Central High—but they were all in the same direction.

Beth, Kayla, and Eliza had already started walking, but Alice stood outside our door waiting for me.

"Where's the lizard?" she demanded.

At the sound of her voice, I felt Squeep! leap inside my backpack.

"Haven't seen him," I said. "Not since last night. Whenever he disappears like that, he usually stays away for days."

"Find him and bring him to me," she said.

"Right," I said, walking faster to get away from her.

"You have one hour," she said.

"Of course," I mumbled.

I hurried ahead and fell in beside my eldest sister.

Eliza ambled along, smiling down at her hand, closely admiring the silver ring. Then she raised it to her mouth and . . . was she whispering to it? Yes, she was *talking* to the ring.

"What's that!" barked Alice, catching up to us.

"Nothing," said Eliza, plunging her hand into her pocket.

"Where did you get that ring?" said Alice.

"None of your business," said Eliza.

"That's *my* ring," said Alice.

"No it's not," said Eliza. "It's Grandma's."

Not wanting any part of this conversation, I hurried ahead of them.

Kayla strolled along staring down at an old issue of *Life* magazine full of photos taken by the Hubble telescope. She studied it whenever there was too much daylight to see outer space through her own little scope.

I could tell, from a minuscule twitching in her face, that she was talking to Alphonso—the two of them probably hot on the trail of a future asteroid or something.

"Kayla," I whispered. "Alice is going to come after me

today. I need to know what she's planning and when. Please tell me."

Kayla ignored me, her face twitching down at a picture of stars.

"What? Are you still mad at me?" I said.

No response.

"Look, I'm sorry about yesterday," I said. "Please . . . this will only take two seconds. Just tell me what Alice is planning so I can take evasive action. All I need is a head start, Kayla. Just a little bit of time."

Kayla gave me the coldest of shoulders. Her bitter expression reminded me of the way she had looked yesterday, right before she juked me.

Remembering that made me angry too.

Rising up with the anger came a thought.

You don't need Kayla to predict things anymore.

"Why not?" I asked myself.

Because, dummy, you have Squeep!

"Squeep! can't predict the future," I thought.

You don't need to know the future. You can pause the present!

CHAPTER 10

DIMITRIUS

The moment I realized it, I wished I hadn't.

When Squeep! held up that flipper, he had offered me all the terrifying powers of the Doorganizer . . . if I only had the courage to use them. And the uses were endless. An unclosable door had opened in my mind, and uninvited schemes crowded through.

Next time Mr. Jamneky unexpectedly called on me in pre-algebra, I could slip out of that moment, figure out the answer in the Doorganizer, and slip back in again without anyone noticing I had gone. I could keep my textbooks in there during tests! I would never have to study or do homework again. No wonder Alice wanted it back so badly.

She would never stop until she had Squeep!

Wait, did I still have Squeep!? I reached behind me and

felt the side of my backpack. Yes, there he was, breathing contentedly. Then I noticed Alice about ten yards back watching me, her eyes going wide with realization.

She nudged Eliza and said something.

Pretending I had just been scratching my side below the backpack, I turned away and walked a little faster, ahead of Kayla, then faster, until I fell in beside my sister Beth.

I glanced back and saw that Alice hadn't followed. She walked twenty yards behind me now and conversed with Eliza.

"What's your deal?" said Beth, eyeing me strangely.

"Huh?" I said. "Oh, nothing. What's going on with you? You look tired."

"I'm exhausted," she said. "I barely slept at all last night."

"Uh-oh," I said. "You're not having Night-Morphs again, are you?"

Night-Morphs, a lingering side-effect of Grandma's experiments on Beth, caused her to transform while she slept into people or things that she dreamed about.

"No, thank heaven," said Beth. "I haven't had one of

those in months. Not since I started the treatment. I was just up late studying for my exam."

"That's a relief," I said.

Beth's Night-Morphs had been an awful ordeal for the entire family, until Dad developed the treatment. Every night Beth had to drink this unpleasant-smelling tea and hypnotize herself before she fell asleep.

Beth and I were silent for the next half a block. Then Kayla, still focused on her magazine, peeled away from the group toward the elementary school. Now I noticed that Alice had left the group as well.

"Where's Alice?" I yelled back at Eliza.

Eliza smiled knowingly and shrugged.

Oh no, I thought.

Alice had slipped away unnoticed to ambush me, I felt certain.

If she came after me, would I dare to hide in the Doorganizer?

No, I needed a better plan.

The twins headed toward the high school. Across from it stood the huge three-story brick box of Wonder Street Middle School.

Alice would expect me to enter as I always did through the double doors on Carnegie Avenue. So, instead, I sprinted toward the line of buses on Wonder Street, where I slipped into the stream of bus kids.

I snuck into the building at the center of a big crowd. Then, hanging a left, I made for the west stairwell and hurried up to the second floor.

I reached room 275, my homeroom, with three minutes to spare. Then realized I still hadn't shaved. So I kept moving down the corridor to the closest second-floor boys' bathroom.

I pushed open the door and headed toward the sinks. Long arms reached down on either side of me. Giant hands clutched my shoulders.

Number 07 from the football team hoisted me high into the air.

"Whoa!" I said. "Hey! What are you . . . Is this about your wallet? I never wanted it! I took it to the office. I didn't take any money, I swear."

"It's not about the wallet," he said, in a shockingly deep voice. Then he yelled out, "I got him!"

I looked around to see who he had yelled to, but we were alone.

The door swung open, and Alice walked into the boys' bathroom.

"Get his backpack, Dimitrius," she said. "And give it to me."

07 peeled the pack from my back like a banana skin. He tossed it to her.

Alice unzipped it and peered inside. Flipping it upside down, she dumped all my books and folders and papers onto the tile floor. There was no sign of Squeep! Alice shook the bag and then crumpled it up.

Spotting something on the tiles, she bent over and picked up . . . another green kazoo. Or maybe the same green kazoo.

She looked furious.

"He comes and goes when he wants to," I said.

"He's stealing from me," she said. "So you're stealing from me."

"I have no control over Squeep!"

"Dunk him in the toilet," she said.

07 lifted me across the room.

"No, wait!" I yelled.

Behind Alice, the door swung open.

An adult!

Never had I been so glad to see a teacher. It was my favorite one too, Mr. Stanley, who taught music. He was everyone's favorite. Always super funny and nice. He had us call him "Stan the Man" instead of Mr. Stanley.

"What the heck's going on in here?" he yelled, seeing the football player holding me so high in the air. "You put him down right now! What on earth do you think yo—"

The word died in his open mouth as Alice rounded to face him.

"Mr. Stanley," she said. "You were never here."

"Okeydoke," he said.

He turned and walked out of the bathroom.

"No, wait!" I cried. "Mr. Stanley, wait! WAIT!"

The door swung shut behind him.

"Stan the Man!" I yelled.

Alice, turning back around, grinned up at me.

"Is it starting to sink in yet?" she said.

CHAPTER 11

ROLL CALL

"There's nowhere you can hide," said Alice. "And no one to protect you. I'll give you ten more minutes to produce the lizard."

She gave 07 a look, and he dropped me.

I landed in a crouch on the tiles.

"Ten minutes," said Alice. "Or else. Come on, Dimitrius."

07, aka Dimitrius, followed her out of the bathroom.

I gathered my books and papers as fast as I could. I grabbed the empty backpack, which felt heavier than it should. I saw that Squeep! had already reappeared inside. He was circular and beckoning me with his flipper.

The homeroom bell rang.

I scooped up my books and papers, set the backpack on top, and carried the whole mess out the door and back to room 275.

There were no assigned seats for homeroom, so I grabbed a spot in the back row, just as Ms. York reached my name in the roll call.

"Conklin, Happy."

"Here!" I said.

I began reorganizing all my folders and sliding them into the backpack, carefully, so as to avoid touching Squeep!'s flipper. Ms. York went on calling the roll. I had everything repacked by the time she got to:

"Melman, Doug."

"Here!" said Doug.

Someone dropped into the seat next to mine.

"I'm here!" said Nev Everly.

She looked out of breath, like she had run to be on time.

Nev had bright-blue eyes. She wore a dress that looked both brand-new and out of a thirty-year-old fashion magazine.

Near her, I always felt two contradictory things: the urgent need to say something and the inability to form words with my brain.

"Mosley, Dana," continued Ms. York.

"Everly, Nevada!" said Nev. "Present!"

Ms. York looked up over her reading glasses.

"Everly, Nevada," said Ms. York. "Tardy."

"Oh please, Ms. York!" said Nev. "You're still calling

roll. You're only on the *M*s. It's not my fault my last name starts with an *E*."

"But it is your fault that you're tardy," said Ms. York.

"How come you never start with *Z*s and move in the other direction?" said Nev. "Mixing it up would be more fair."

Some of the kids laughed. I decided that this would be a good moment to say something funny, like . . .

I couldn't think of anything.

I looked at my desk. Squeep!'s flipper was poking out of my backpack, reaching for me.

I moved my hand toward the flipper.

The moment before my finger touched it, I thought of something funny to say.

"She's on their side," I could say. "Ms. York begins with a *Y*."

Not hilarious, but funny enough to say.

Only I didn't say it, because I wasn't in the classroom anymore.

I was back in the worst place I'd ever been, having a catastrophic breakdown.

CHAPTER 12

OWL-HEADED CRYSTAL MONSTERS

Mentally, I knew the trick of surviving in the Door-ganizer: take deep breaths and stay calm.

So I told myself, "Don't panic. It's okay."

But when your body knows it SHOULD panic, your mind saying not to only makes matters worse.

Body: "Everything's gone crazy! Panic! Panic!"

Mind: "Don't panic. It's okay."

Body: "Great, the mind's gone crazy too! PANIC! PANIC! PANIC!"

Dad had been right about one thing. Just because I'd been in extra-dimensional space-time didn't mean I understood it. And "fear of the unknown" is a picnic compared to the terror of the incomprehensible.

I looked down at the mountain of junk beneath my feet: kids' desks, teachers' desks, blackboards, audio/visual equipment, globes, wastebaskets, pencil sharpeners, industrial-size cafeteria equipment, and thousands of other things Alice had stolen from the school throughout her sixth- and seventh-grade years.

I noticed Squeep! floating somehow in midair beside me, his body still circular, his flipper reaching toward me.

I reached out and touched it, hoping he meant to take me back out of this place.

But he didn't bite down on the tip of his tail. Instead, his circular body started rotating clockwise, moving us both through time.

Of all the awful creepy feelings in the Doorganizer, time travel was the worst. It could so easily lead to catastrophe.

If you went backward, the months and years could fly by until you actually saw Alice stealing things in reverse. You could watch millions of blur-fast Alices buzzing around the junk piles like bees, dismantling the place until there was nothing left but a single baby Alice hiding the first thing she ever stole: one of Grandma's cookies.

But we weren't moving toward the past. Instead, Squeep! pulled me into the future. I know now that he would have had to rotate counterclockwise to go backward. He wasn't taking me to the birth of the Doorganizer. He meant to show me its death.

I had no idea how far or fast we moved forward through

time—seconds? days? years?—because I couldn't see any variation at all in our surroundings.

Until everything changed at once.

The lights went out. They came back on in flashing strobes as I heard enormous sounds of destruction all around me.

I looked up into the darkness to see hundreds of pieces of paper drifting down through mobile beams of light.

Searchlights. I didn't like the look of them—something about how they moved and bobbed . . .

I snatched one of the drifting papers from the air. Upon it, I saw maybe the last thing I expected. A picture of Grandma and me.

Shoving the paper into my pocket, I heard a massive:
CRUNCH!

An enormous crystal foot slammed into the ground.
A barrel-hinged ankle turned and then hoisted the foot
back up.

I lifted my gaze and saw a huge portal, opening onto
another world.

Then I heard another crunching foot-slam.

Tilting my head farther back, I looked up a tower of crystal legs, past its torso, and into the monster's blinding single eye. Its head looked like a giant cycloptic owl perched on its crystal torso.

It spoke—an earsplitting blare.

I couldn't understand most of it, but I did pick out the words "surrender, Happy."

I turned and sprinted away. But after only a few strides, I tripped over a tuba Alice must have stolen out of the music room.

Falling, I rolled under a grand piano and across a pile of sheet music.

Peeking out from the other side of the piano, I looked up at a tree-size crystal spike falling straight toward my face.

I dove away, down an embankment of textbooks. Mid-dive, upside down, I saw the spiked arm of the giant creature plunge into the piano.

But instead of smashing the keyboard into matchsticks, the spike punctured the surface of space-time.

A bursting white light blasted the creature off its feet and into the air, where it got sucked into a black dot at the center of everything.

This dot, I knew, was the micro black hole itself—somehow made visible . . . and growing larger.

The entire Doorganizer shifted and seemed to deflate.

I grabbed hold of a desk leg and clung to it like it was a life preserver.

White light fizzled from the puncture wound over the piano. Then something small popped through it. An arm. A kid's arm. A girl's arm. Then a shoulder. Then a head with long, flowing, wavy brown hair.

Nev Everly looked around in astonishment.

Her eyes landed on me.

"Grab on to something!" I yelled.

Nev grabbed the underside of the piano just as the rest of her came flipping in from the outer world. Her school chair rolled in after her, followed by her desk, which ripped the white opening wider.

All at once a crowd of kids, chairs, and tables tumbled in. Dana Mosley, a teacher's desk, Jake Harrison, Mr. Stanley, Doug Melman, a door, and Davina Tyler whirled off toward the growing central black dot.

After them, a full blast of kids and school poured in.

Broken floorboards, a wall of lockers, a clock reading 11:15, fluorescent light fixtures still attached to chunks of the ceiling. Everything rushed behind Nev like a passing freight train. Brick walls, whole classrooms, cars, and trees. Tumbling school buses. All ripping it open even wider.

Nev, clinging to the edge of the piano, dangled at the cusp of a growing chasm where whole houses, highways, and buildings fell churning in massive dust clouds. Then entire forests, mountains, cities, roaring seas, the bulging Earth itself pushed in and funneled toward the central, growing black hole.

"Nev," I said, reaching my hand toward her.

"Happy!" she shouted back.

I stretched out my fingers.

I felt something crawling on my shoulder. Squeep!

scurried up my arm and onto my hand. Looping his body, he spun counterclockwise. As time reversed at hyperspeed, Squeep! bit down onto the tip of his tail.

"Nev," I said.

"Yes?" said the girl seated next to me in homeroom.

"Norton, Andre," said Ms. York, still calling the attendance roll.

"Here," said Andre.

"Nowlan, Philip," said Ms. York.

Everyone sat at his or her desk. The Earth was still here, unharmed, uncrushed. The kids, the desks, the classroom, the planet, Ms. York, me, Nev.

She stared at me, because I had just said her name aloud.

"What?" she said. "What is it?"

"Uh . . ."

CHAPTER 13

THE TORN PAPER

"Uh . . . ," I said, feeling a wave of euphoria.

We were all alive!

"What?" said Nev, smiling now, because I was smiling.

"Uh," I said. "Can I borrow a pencil?"

"Oh . . . sure," she said, lifting up a shoulder bag the same color as her watch band. "Do you need it just right now or for the whole day?"

"Just for right now," I said, glancing into my own backpack.

Squeep! wasn't in there anymore.

"Here you go," said Nev.

I took the pencil from her and stared down at it blankly, still trying to figure out what had just happened. I had watched the entire Earth destroyed in front of me, but now it was all back. As real as this pencil, which seemed like the most real thing I'd ever held in my hand. A Ticonderoga. The sort of pencil that smells like the forest.

"Thank you," I said to Nev, and also to the universe. I felt the idiotic smile still smeared across my face, but I didn't care. We were alive!

"No problem," said Nev. "Your name's Happy, right? . . . Can I ask you something?"

"Sure," I said, grinning at her. Why had I ever felt afraid to talk to this girl? There were scary things out there, but she wasn't one of them.

"Are you in the school play or something?" she said.

"No," I said. "I didn't even know about it."

"Then why are you made up like that?" she said.

"Made up?" I said.

"You're wearing stage makeup," she said, "to look like you have a five-o'clock shadow."

I touched the stubble on my grinning face.

"Oh this," I said. "It's not makeup. I just forgot to shave this morning."

"Oh, yeah right," she said. "Don't even try to tell me that's real."

"Sure it's real," I said. "I have a beard."

"What? Shut up." She laughed.

"Ask anyone," I said, grinning. "They all used to call me Beard Boy and do the Make-Beard-Boy-Cry Dance."

She burst out laughing, and so did I.

Would this have embarrassed me before? Now it seemed like the funniest thing in the world.

"Wait, wait," she said, narrowing her eyes. "This is a joke you play on people. There's no way you already shave every day."

"I shave three times a day," I said. "And if I don't, I end up looking like the world's smallest hillbilly."

She laughed again, throwing her head back. Her laugh was ridiculous. A *he-he* from the back of her throat that made me laugh too.

I remembered now how I had wanted to make her laugh, and why.

"Do you have a lab partner in science yet?" I asked.

"No," she said.

"Do you want to be my lab partner?"

"Sure. We can do our project on why you lie about having a beard."

I shrugged, smiling. I figured she had taken it all as a joke, but that was okay. Being lab partners with her didn't seem like such a big important deal anymore.

"How do I text you?" she asked.

"I don't have my own phone," I said. "But you can email me."

"Okay," she said.

I pulled a piece of paper from my pocket and tore it in half.

We both wrote our emails with her Ticonderoga pencil.

Nev joined the kids getting up to go.

"See you later," she said.

I nodded.

I didn't want to leave until I had found Squeep!

He wasn't in my backpack, but I saw he had left a doodad behind for me there. A nacho chip . . . the exact same nacho chip from before.

I looked down at the piece of paper, where Nev had written her email.

I unfolded it. On the other side, I saw half of the image of Grandma and me, with all the different languages, that I had taken from . . .

It had all been real. And yet, somehow, none of it had happened.

As I puzzled over this in the emptying classroom, a small girl in a yellow headband came tearing in. Kayla, of all people.

Out of breath, she had clearly sprinted here from the elementary school, though her skin wasn't flushed. Her face looked as white as fresh mozzarella, and her glossy eyes spilled tears.

"Hap!" she said, panting. "Oh my God, it's so awful! I couldn't see it before . . . I wasn't looking on Earth. I was

looking in space, *way* in the future. But it happens here! *Right* here. In the present. Today! Really soon. Oh no . . . I can't even say it!"

"A black hole," I said. "A black hole opens up."

She looked astonished.

"How do you know?" she said.

"I just watched it happen," I said. "I might . . . I might have caused it."

PART 2

THE BLACK HOLE

CHAPTER 14

BLIND SPOT

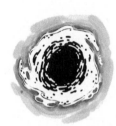

I showed Kayla the ripped flyer, hoping she would attach to it and follow it back a few minutes to witness the catastrophe for herself.

"I can't *see* into that place," she reminded me.

"Oh, right," I said.

To Kayla and Alphonso, any event in the Doorganizer happened in an enormous blind spot.

So I told her. I described the crazy lights, the jagged

hole into a futuristic world, and the owl-headed crystal monster. How it yelled my name and the word "surrender" before stabbing the piano. I told her about the explosion of white light and the growing black hole pulling everything in—the classroom, the school, our town, what seemed like the whole world.

"Then everything spun backward," I said, "really fast, for an instant, and then . . . none of it had happened. I was back in class. I felt sure it had all been a hallucination. I still feel certain that none of it happened."

"None of it has happened yet," said Kayla. "You were two hours and thirty-seven minutes in the future. At 11:15 this morning a black hole will open up right here. Dead smack in the center of your school."

"Well, we gotta DO something!" I said, a high-pitched trill creeping into my voice. "We gotta pull the fire alarm and evacuate the school or—"

"It's a black hole, Hap," said Kayla. "Where are we going to evacuate to, Alpha Centauri? . . . Okay, take a breath. You're on the verge of going into shock. Take a deep breath."

I did. And a clearer thought struck me.

"Squeep!" I said. "We need to find Squeep! He's been trying to tell me something for days. It must be about this."

"Is Squeep! the portal?" asked Kayla.

"Dad says he can't be," I said. "But he goes in and out whenever he wants. Also, when I ask Squeep! where the Doorganizer is, he gives me this."

I handed Kayla the nacho chip. She stared at it, her face quivering.

Then she groaned in frustration.

"If I could only see into that place," she said. "Okay, we need Squeep! Where do you usually find him?"

"I can never find him!" I said. "He always finds me."

"Right," she said. "Where does he expect you to be right now?"

"Heading to my first-hour class," I said. "Science."

"So let's get over there," she said, but then clamped down on my arm so hard it hurt. "No, wait! Somebody else is looking for Squeep! too."

"Yeah," I said. "Alice. I tried to tell you that earlier, but you—"

"We can't let her catch him," said Kayla. "We can't let her catch *you* especially! Okay . . . Hap, you stand right there, on that spot . . ."

Uh-oh, I thought. It was never a good sign when Kayla started giving me step-by-step choreography.

"Wait right there until you hear the desk break, then run for that door and go straight to your next class. Stay wherever Squeep! would expect you to be, so he can find you. He's afraid of Alice, so steer clear of her."

"Desk break?" I said.

"Yes, then run out *that* door."

She pointed to the exit at the front of the class but stared toward the other door at the rear. Alice and Dimitrius came walking through.

"Kayla!" said Alice, glaring. "What are you doing here? Are you in on this with him? Are you stealing from me too?"

"No, Alice," I said. "You've got to listen to us! Something really bad is about to—"

"Don't bother, Hap," said Kayla. "She's back in her obsessive mania. Nothing we say will make any difference. She won't even hear us."

"*You're* the one with the mania!" yelled Alice. "You're the ones trying to steal from me!"

"Should I grab them both?" said Dimitrius, striding toward us between a row of desks.

"Yes," said Alice. "But watch out for her."

"Watch out for *her*?" laughed Dimitrius.

Then his expression changed as Kayla glided upward, stepping lightly off a chair, to run across the desktops straight toward him.

"Careful," said Alice as Kayla hurtled closer. "Watch her . . ."

Dimitrius shot out an arm the length of Kayla's whole body to grab her. As his fingertips touched her shirt, she twirled sideways, landing atop the next row while Dimitrius, overreaching his balance, fell gut-first onto a desk, which shrieked out *CRAAAAANCH!* as it collapsed, cracking like a nut between his body and the floor.

A desk breaking. That meant I should do something.

Kayla and Alice glared at each other over the wreck of Dimitrius.

Run, I remembered.

Turning on my heels, I dashed out into the hallway.

CHAPTER 15

LIKE AN ARROW

Running, I carried this light, slithery feeling in my stomach.

My science class wasn't far, only a ways around the next corner.

Had the first-hour bell rung yet? Glancing up at a hallway clock, I saw I still had about fifty seconds.

The sight of the clock made the slithering in my stomach lurch. I had just seen it, this clock, along with part of the wall and a hunk of the ceiling, fly past me inside the Doorganizer. My mind's eye recalled now the full, vivid, stinging picture. The clock whirled within a mess of papers, books, and students—its face, caught at 11:15, beside a kid's face frozen in astonishment as he watched his ripping brown lunch bag eject its contents.

A crazy old joke, "*Time flies like an arrow. Fruit flies*

like a banana," escaped from some asylum in my mind to run madly through my thoughts.

"Stop it!" I yelled silently. "Do not go crazy. You can still prevent this from ever happening."

Where was Squeep! now that I needed him?

Wait, was that really our big plan? How was Squeep! supposed to stop a black hole? What was he going to do, hand it a nacho chip?

But the nacho chip must have *meant* something, like "seashell" meant "Doorganizer." Squeep!'s doodads had been warnings, or maybe instructions. I still had some in the side pocket of my backpack and the Doodad Decoder in my notebook. Maybe Squeep! had already given me the whole solution, if I could be smart enough and stay sane enough to understand it.

The first-hour bell rang.

Time flies like an arrow. Walking into the classroom, I saw kids still milling about—several the same ones I'd seen sucked into the black hole minutes earlier, or hours later, depending on how you looked at it. *Fruit flies like a banana.*

Willow Johansen stood with Lacy and Paisley, the two little friends who followed her around laughing at her jokes and doing whatever she told them to. These three girls had so ridiculed and bad-mouthed me over the years that I normally found the sight of them slightly disgusting.

But now everything looked different.

Willow, Lacy, and Paisley weren't repulsive little brats. They were unique, extraordinary, and precious little brats, who had as much a right as anyone to not be vaporized into a black hole before gym class.

Nearing them, I noticed Willow cradling something green in her hands, while Lacy and Paisley giggled. When I realized what Willow held, I almost screamed.

"You found him," I said, reaching out for Squeep! "You found my lizard."

"Get away," said Willow, pulling back from me. "He's not yours."

Before I could contradict her, I realized that she was right. This wasn't Squeep! Though the same type of lizard, this one looked more . . . bloated.

"He's my lab partner's," said Willow.

"Lab partner?" I said.

"Actually, Conklin," said a voice, "that's me. What did he actually do, Willow?"

Felix strolled up and stood beside her.

"He tried to grab the Mighty Thor," said Willow. "He said that it was *his* lizard."

"Holy crow, Conklin," said Felix. "Are you actually crazy? What is it with you and lizards, anyway?"

"Time flies like an arrow," I said, accidentally out loud.

"Huh?" Willow laughed. "Have you flipped out or something?"

As I turned away and headed toward my desk, I heard Felix say:

"You know he actually has an imaginary lizard?"

"What!" laughed the girls.

"He thinks it's a real lizard," said Felix, "but it's actually just a seashell that he carries around in a bowling ball bag."

Squeals of laughter.

Feeling dizzy, I dropped into my assigned seat by the window.

"Enough!" said Ms. Prince, our science teacher. She turned around from where she had been writing on the whiteboard. "You girls settle down. I'm not going to let anyone do any special projects unless they act responsibly. That means finding your assigned seat, right now."

I looked into the backpack on my desk. No Squeep!

Maybe I *was* going crazy. I felt like I might burst into hysterical laughter or tears or both. Kayla had said I was "on the verge of shock."

I needed to take deep breaths and remember what to do . . . do . . .

"Doodads," I said, reaching into my backpack. "Do the doodads, do the doodads, do the doodads. Time flies like an arrow."

I opened my math notebook to the "Doodad Decoder" and reread it.

Unzipping the side pocket of my bag, I took out the three I had with me. The bottle cap, the chocolate Easter egg, and the quarter.

I picked up the bottle cap and turned it over in my hand.

It was from one of Kayla's Tamarindo sodas and . . .

I smacked a palm to my head for being so stupid.

The bottle cap *meant* "Kayla." It repre-sented her. Nobody else drank that kind of soda. Squeep! had wanted me to tell Kayla . . . to tell her what?

I picked up the quarter and the Eas-ter egg. Squeep! had always delivered these two as a pair. Every other doodad was singular, but the coin and the chocolate egg meant something together, in combination.

Quarter plus egg equals . . . what?

Ms. Prince had stopped talking. Kids moved about the classroom.

I stared at the coin, turning it over in my hand—a state quarter with picture of a sailboat and the words "Rhode Island" on the back.

Easter boat? No. Twenty-five-cent egg? No. Chocolate George Washington? No. Time flies like an arrow? No, time flies *love* an arrow. I wondered if Alphonso the bee had ever met the time flies.

"*Howdy, lab partner*," said a country-western accent.

Nev Everly dropped down into the seat next to mine.

"So," she said, "what's the plan for our big science project?"

"Fruit flies like a banana," I said.

"Hmm . . . ," said Nev. "Well, I suppose they would. They *are* fruit flies, and a banana's fruit. I don't think we're going win any Nobel Prizes with that one, Happy."

She looked down at the doodads on my desk.

"What's that stuff for?"

"Oh, this?" I said. "It's like a riddle. Want to help me solve it?"

She scowled and smiled at the same time.

"Okay, buddy," she said. "What's the riddle?"

I slid the Easter egg and the quarter toward her.

"Gross," she said. "Is that from *last* Easter?"

"These two things are like a crossword clue for something," I said. "The quarter, plus the egg equals . . . what?"

She picked up the quarter and examined it.

She frowned down at the Easter egg without picking it up. Then she looked back at the quarter.

"Huh," she said. "Maybe Easter Island?"

"What's that?" I said.

"You know, Easter Island. It's in the South Pacific. It's got all those big heads on it with long faces?"

"I've never heard of it," I said.

"I'm sure you've seen pictures," she said. "Hold on . . ."

She took out her phone and tapped something into an image search.

"Easter Island . . . ," I said, stroking my beard.

Nev glanced up at me from her phone. Her eyes grew wide.

She leaned in really close to me.

"Holy geez," she whispered. "It's longer. That thing is actually *growing* from your *face.*"

"I told you," I said, laughing at her amazement.

"I can't believe that's real," she said.

She lifted her hand.

"Sorry," she said, "but do you mind if I . . . ?"

"Nah," I said. "Go ahead."

"Wicked," she said, running her fingers along my cheek. "It grows *that* fast?"

"Yeah," I said, feeling a little self-conscious. "But I usually shave it."

"Why?"

"'Cause if I don't, you know, it weirds everybody out." I glanced back at Willow, Lacy, and Paisley. They weren't laughing now, but staring in openmouthed astonishment at the sight of Nev Everly touching my beard.

From somewhere out the window, I heard distant sirens.

"You shouldn't shave this," said Nev.

"I have to," I said. "Otherwise I'll look like Rip van Winkle."

"You should trim it, not shave it," she said. "If it was a little longer than this, that would look so righteous. Do you have a beard trimmer?"

"No," I said.

"You can get good ones really cheap," she said. "I see them all the time in the thrift stores."

"Is that where you get your clothes?" I said.

"Yeah," she said. "Or vintage stuff from online. I don't wear anything new."

"Why not?"

"All the good stuff's from the past."

The sirens had grown so loud kids were getting up to look out the windows.

"Okay," said Ms. Prince. "Everyone get back in your seats."

No one listened. Outside two squad cars and two black SUVs screeched up onto Carnegie Avenue.

I knew those SUVs.

"That's a lot of cops," said Nev.

"It's the FBI," I said.

"Why do you say that?" she asked.

I wondered how they'd found out. Had Kayla told them? That seemed unlikely. The agents getting out of the first SUV all wore suits, the ones from the second wore blue windbreakers with the letters "FBI" printed in yellow.

"Whoa," said Nev. "You're right. *Los Federales!*"

Among the FBI in suits, I spotted an agent half as tall as all the others. Good old Detective Frank Segar. Now I knew they had come for me.

Or . . . maybe they hadn't. Instead of moving in on our building, they headed across the street, toward Central High.

Kids made the *ooh* sound kids make when somebody else is in trouble. I thought about Eliza and Beth.

"How did you know it was the FBI?" said Nev.

"That's a long story," I said.

"*Well, supposin' you tell it, boy!*" Nev, slipping back into the country-western accent, made me laugh.

Hadn't she been about to show me something on her phone?

A blaring noise, louder than the sirens, came from the PA speaker at the front of the classroom. *Bung-bong-bung* went the chimes, followed by the voice of Principal Kellogg.

"Attention, students. Attention, students," said the voice. "Would Happy Conklin please report to the office. Happy Conklin to the office, please."

"Ooh," went the kids. Everyone stared at me.

"Okay, stop that," said Ms. Prince. "Happy, you're excused."

I sat there trying to remember what I had been trying to remember.

"Easter Island," I whispered to Nev. "Did you find a picture?"

Nev held her phone below the desktop, so Ms. Prince wouldn't see she had it out in class. She unlocked the screen with her thumb.

"Get moving, Happy," said Ms. Prince. "Or should I call someone to escort you down?"

"Ooh," went the class.

But I had no attention for anything beyond the image on Nev's phone.

In a blue ocean, on a green island, stood many enormous black sculptures of heads. And each face looked just like the Galactic Emperor's.

CHAPTER 16

THE HOT SEAT

I sat paralyzed, until I heard Ms. Prince say something about calling for a security guard to escort me.

"I'm going," I said, gathering my stuff into my backpack.

"Thanks," I said to Nev.

"Sure," she said. "Good luck?"

Kids continued to "ooh" as I walked toward the door. Felix stared up at me, shaking his head.

Out in the hallway, I didn't make it ten yards before I had to lean against a wall of lockers to keep from falling over as the full weight of my doom sunk in.

What had Squeep! been so desperate to tell me? That I was a fugitive from the Galactic Empire. Not only were they hunting me through the Doorganizer, but they also knew about Earth. They'd been here! So even if we figured out some way to stop the black hole, they'd find me eventually. And they wouldn't think twice about obliterating our entire solar system just to kill me . . . and Grandma.

Wanting to kill *her*, that I understood. Grandma was trying to overthrow the Emperor and take his place as ruler of the galaxy.

But what had *I* ever done to him?

"Hey, bubba!" said a gruff voice. A school security guard walked toward me. "Aren't you supposed to be headed for the office?"

It was the older, white-bearded guard. The one all the kids called "Santa Claus" behind his back.

"I'm going," I said. "I just need a second."

"Get moving, bubba," he said.

"Okay, okay."

I started toward the stairs.

Santa Claus followed me down two flights and across the first floor to the school office. Along the way, I tried to formulate some sort of brilliant plan. But all I could think of was to keep squeezing my backpack so I'd know if Squeep! reappeared inside.

Where is he? I kept thinking. *And where's Kayla?*

As I entered the outer office, the secretaries hushed each other and looked at me.

I glanced at the closed door that read "Principal Kellogg."

In one of the waiting chairs along the wall, known as

the "hot seats," sat the biggest kid in the school—not Dimitrius but the even larger eighth-grade football player Kenny "Moose-O" Caruso. He and the team had all worn their jerseys today, which meant they had a game this afternoon, if there still was any such thing as "this afternoon."

Sorry, sports fans, but today's game has been called on account of the Earth vanishing like a dust bunny up a vacuum cleaner.

"He's here," a secretary said into her phone. "Yes, uh-huh."

A moment later, the door opened.

"You," said Principal Kellogg, pointing at me. "Get in here."

I had never been in her office before. The first thing I noticed was the PA system microphone on an old-fashioned switchboard of lights and toggles. A small trio of chimes sat in front of it. What I had always assumed to be a digital sound effect had actually been the principal herself hitting three xylophone pieces with a little wooden mallet. Weird.

Turning into the room, I saw something far stranger.

Dimitrius, a fresh white bandage on his forehead, stood *behind* the principal's desk. Before I could even try to make sense of this, I looked down and saw my sister Alice sitting in the principal's chair, her hands folded in front of her on the desk and—most disturbing of all—a big flashing smile pressed across her face.

"*Eee-yipe*," I said.

"Happy, dear brother." Alice grinned. "Come. Come and have a seat."

She gestured at the chair across the desk from her.

I looked from Alice to Principal Kellogg.

"Oh, Ms. Kellogg," said Alice. "We'll need the room a moment. Come back in five."

"Look, Alice," said the principal. "I think this has gone too far. You know I need to—"

"Ms. Kellogg, please," said Alice. "Don't make this difficult. I would hate to have to make my own announcement over the PA system."

"No!" said the principal, her face flushing a deep, cloudy red. "You wouldn't . . . You . . ."

"We'll only be a moment," said Alice.

A lost look came into Principal Kellogg's eyes as she turned around and walked out of her own office, shutting the door behind her.

"Come, Hap, sit," said Alice, still grinning insanely. "Can Dimitrius get you a soda or a juice or something?"

Dimitrius stared down at me with murder in his eyes.

"No, I'm good," I said.

"Well, just let me know," said Alice, smiling. "Anything you want. Anything for family. We *are* family, brother. Never forget it. We're on the same team. We've fought the same fights. We should be working together here. That's what Kayla doesn't understand. I only want what's best for everyone. What's best for you, what's best for me, what's best for the lizard."

"You know the FBI's here?" I said.

"No, they're across the street," said Alice. "That

situation is contained at the high school. It doesn't concern us. That's between Beth and the FBI."

"Beth?" I said. "What happened to Beth?"

"She's fine," said Alice. "We're not here to talk about Beth."

"Did she have a Night-Morph at school?"

"I said we're not here to TALK ABOUT BETH!" Alice slammed her fists onto the principal's desk. I had never seen such madness in her face before. I had to get out of there.

Just agree to whatever she says, I thought, *and then run.*

Crazy-eyed, Alice took deep breaths and, by degrees, the smile crept back onto her face.

"Now, *you* found something," she said. "It belongs to me, but you did find it. And I'll show my appreciation for that with a big reward for you. We'll go into my closet together, and you can take as much as you want of whatever you want. I think that's more than fair, Hap."

"Okay!" I said. "Absolutely."

"Don't give me 'absolutely,'" she said. "I don't want 'absolutely.' I want the lizard! And I want him right now."

"Sure," I said. "I just need to go to my locker to get him."

"Nice try," said Alice. "But we've already searched your locker."

"Well, of course, he's not *in* my locker," I said. "But I

have to be *at* my locker to, you know, summon him up from the Doorganizer."

Alice stared at me.

"Dimitrius," said Alice, "would you and Moose-O Caruso please escort my brother to his locker?"

"Moose-O?" I said.

"These two will be your chaperones until I have the lizard," said Alice. "And I *will* have him, Happy. I've got all the security guards hunting for him now, all the janitors, *and* the football team. I will have the lizard. The only question is you. Will you be rewarded? Or will you get hurt? And since you're my brother, I'd really hate to see you get hurt."

CHAPTER 17

MY BIG SUPERPOWER

They marched me out of the office like a prisoner, Dimitrius on my left, Moose-O Caruso on my right.

I scrambled to think of an escape plan. What clever lie could I tell them? What tricky diversion? What fancy dance move?

But when I looked up at the hallway clock, I saw that the time for scheming was over. It was 10:13.

Time flies like an arrow, crossed my thoughts, *and so should you.*

The only possible plan was to run faster than they could.

To turn and sprint.

And since there were no other options, I had to stop thinking about it and just go ahead and—

The moment I took off, I felt one of their grasping

fingers slip across the back of my shirt. I pushed on harder, bursting through the stairwell doors, climbing, forcing every bit of my will into the same singular idea of:

Faster! Faster! Faster!

Yet, as big as they were, the football players overtook me.

Halfway up the second flight, Dimitrius caught hold of my wrist and yanked me backward, twisting my arm into some pretzel hold that turned my legs limp and fogged my vision with tears.

Dimitrius struck me in the head—an open-handed blow, but so powerful I saw a flash of blackness and went reeling around in a daze.

Moose-O found my pain hilarious.

"Haw-haw-haw," he laughed over me.

I recalled hearing somewhere that Moose-O had inflicted so many football injuries they named a wing of Children's Hospital after him.

Probably just a rumor.

"Haw-haw! Hold up." He laughed. "Hold up. Let me do one."

Moose-O wheeled way back and swung his limp, pot-roast-size hand into the side of my head.

Each finger felt like a tire iron. This time the flash of blackness glittered with stars as my stomach opened vomit negotiations with my throat.

For a moment, I thought I'd gone deaf. Then sound returned in the form of those two idiots laughing their heads off over me.

"We should get moving," laughed Dimitrius.

"Aw come on," said Moose-O. "Just a couple more."

"Well," said Dimitrius, "okay, but just a *couple* more."

"No more," I wheezed. "No more, please."

"Excuse me," said a girl, skipping past us up the stairs along our right.

I was so punch-drunk that Dimitrius recognized Kayla before I did.

"That's HER!" he bellowed. "Get that one! Get her!"

Moose-O sprang like a prehistoric beast.

Up the stairs he flew, arms wheeling, overtaking my sister in two leaping strides. Kayla, to my surprise, fell into a crouching ball and rolled backward down the steps. Moose-O lunged down for her so hard that his face cracked the banister in half.

His head bounced off it like a bowling ball, swinging his huge body backward, tipping the whole heap of him over, straight at us.

Dimitrius dove left.

I stood frozen, watching Kayla spring up backward, both her feet kicking into the falling flank of Moose-O, pushing the trajectory of his mass a few inches to the right so that he plowed straight into the diving Dimitrius. The two giants rolled down the steps in a wildly kicking pile of limbs.

"Move," said Kayla, grabbing hold of my wrist.

We ran up the next flight and into the second-floor hallway, where Kayla pulled me into an empty art room.

"Your shaving cream and your razor," she said. "Hurry!"

"Where the heck have you been?" I said.

"I had to run back to Acorn Lane for something," she said, opening her yellow backpack. "Quick, give me your razor."

"To the elementary school?" I said, unzipping the outside pocket of my bag. "Why'd you— Holy cow! You found him! You found—"

But then I realized the lizard she had taken from her backpack wasn't Squeep! This lizard wore green glasses and had a mustache.

"That's Florida Pete!" I said.

"Shh! Yeah. Now give me your razor. We have to shave him so Alice thinks he's Squeep!"

"You can't shave a mustache that thick with a razor," I said. "You need to start with . . ."

Scanning the room, I dashed over and grabbed a pair of art scissors out of the wooden rack. Then I ran back, crouched down beside Kayla, and began snipping away at Pete's mustache.

"Am I supposed to understand why we're doing this?" I said.

"Squeep!'s afraid of Alice," said Kayla. "I think that's why he's staying away. If we convince her she's already caught him, it will be safe for the real Squeep! to come back. Then he'll help us stop the black hole."

"Is that your real plan, Kayla?" I said. "Or just the one that I'm supposed to believe?"

"Hey, it will get Alice off *your* back too," she said. "You need to be in your 10:50 music class. That's the most important thing. We can't have Alice interfering with that."

"Yeah, but a decoy lizard?" I said, still snipping away at Pete's mustache. "Why can't you just convince Alice of the truth?"

"You saw her. When she's like this, the only way to tell her the truth is to lie to her, and the only way to lie to her is to tell her the truth."

Kayla took the green Perfect-O-Specs glasses off Florida Pete and folded them into her pants pocket.

"Won't he turn back into Pete the wrestler without those?" I asked.

"Not if the world ends in forty minutes," said Kayla.

Having trimmed Pete's mustache down to stubble, I reached into the pocket of my backpack for the shaving cream and razor.

I glimpsed the doodads inside.

"Hey, Kayla," I said as I applied a careful bracket of shaving cream below Pete's nose and around his mouth. "I figured out something that Squeep! tried to tell me earlier. Do you know about Easter Island?"

"Yeah," she said glumly. "The Galactic Empire visited it nine hundred and thirty-one years ago."

"So you knew that?" I said. "That they know about Earth."

"Sure," she said. "But we've never been important to them. We're too primitive. Our solar system's just a backwater to the Empire. Or, at least, we *were* up until now . . . I guess Grandma must have started her war."

"But I didn't start any wars!" I said. "Why are they after me? Why's my face on that flyer too?"

"I don't know," said Kayla. "I can't see across the whole galaxy. Although . . . you *were* Grandma's partner up there."

"For *one* wrestling match," I said. "They're going to vaporize us all because of one stupid wrestling match?"

"Let's just stop the black hole," said Kayla. "After that we can worry about the Galactic Empire. You almost done?"

"Yeah," I said, giving Pete one final stroke with the razor.

Kayla examined his face while I wiped off the extra shaving cream.

"You *are* good at that," she said.

"Well, I ought to be by now," I said. "It's my one big superpower.

"Where to now?" I said, following her back out into the hallway.

"You're going to give Pete to a security guard," said Kayla, handing me the lizard, "who'll bring him to Alice. I'll deal with her football flunkies. Then we'll rendezvous outside your music room after the bell."

"Football flunkies?" I said.

"Yes, and they're about to spot me. Get back against the wall so they don't see you. They come in, you go out. Understand?"

"I don't know," I said, backing up against the wall. "*Do* I understand?"

Kayla, turning away from me, struck the pose of an innocent daydreaming little girl as a shout of "There she is!" came from the doors to my left.

They burst open. Dimitrius and Moose-O charged in, running straight for Kayla—Moose-O's face still a mess from its encounter with the banister.

As the doors closed behind them, I slipped out and ran up the steps toward the third floor.

CHAPTER 18

CATCHING UP WITH PETE

Wait, but had Kayla told me to run *up* the stairs?

All she'd actually said was to give Pete to a security guard. Why had I assumed she meant one on the third floor and not the first?

I looked down at the lizard in my hands. Pete's tongue flicked out around his upper mouth, searching for the missing mustache.

"Sorry about that, old buddy," I said, pushing through the door to the third-floor hallway. "It's only temporary... I think. Look, I know you're retired these days. But you need to come back for one last job. We wouldn't be asking for your help if it wasn't so important."

Pete blinked skeptically.

"Fair enough," I said. "We're not exactly 'asking,' are we? But I promise that your part in this will be easy. You won't have to turn back into a human, or wrestle, or kill anybody. In fact, I'd prefer if you didn't do any of those things. We just need you to stay a lizard so Alice thinks you're Squeep! See, because that way . . ."

Pete stared at me.

"Okay, to be honest, I don't completely understand this plan myself," I said. "But Kayla's usually right about these things. Although, in this case . . . I mean, she can't see into the Doorganizer any more than I can. So she's probably using a lot of guesswork here . . . Anyway, my point is—"

Up ahead, the door to the boys' bathroom swung open.

I sidestepped from view, flattening myself against the wall.

"Shh," I said, hushing Pete.

A security guard came out of the boys' room—not Santa Claus, but a younger one whose funny nickname I didn't know.

I felt certain this must be the guard Kayla had meant. I decided to walk up and hand him Pete.

But I grew a lot less certain when I noticed that this security guard was already carrying a lizard.

Squeep!? No, the eyes were too bulgy, their expression too dull, the body too bloated for it to be Squeep! This was the Mighty Thor.

The guard carried him out of the boys' room in a nest of wet paper towels, as though he had just taken Thor out of a water bath in the sink. The lizard disappeared from view as the guard turned toward the central stairs.

I followed quickly but stopped after a few steps, realizing that I had no idea what to do next.

Run up to him with Pete? And say what? "Care for another?"

I watched the guard turn right and vanish down the central stairway.

What would Kayla want me to do?

I looked down into my hand, as though Pete might advise me.

"Any ideas?" I said.

Pete looked up in alarm, and then was whisked from my palm entirely.

"Give him back!" said Felix, yanking Pete away.

"No, Felix," I said.

"What is actually wrong with you, Conklin?" said Felix, clutching Pete like a rescued baby. "I leave him for a minute to do his business and you actually steal him?"

"I wasn't stealing him," I said, stepping forward, "because that's not the Mighty Thor. Look at him!"

"Get away from us!" said Felix, stepping back.

"It's Pete! Pete the lizard. Not Thor. Give him back to me!"

"You're actually crazy, Conklin!" Felix backed away. "You're a crazy insane maniac."

"I just shaved him," I said. "With my razor. How could I shave Thor's mustache? Thor doesn't even have one!"

"Get away!" yelled Felix, swinging his backpack as I advanced. With his other hand he held Pete far behind him and out of my reach.

"He's not even bloated!" I said, dodging the backpack. "Look at him. It's not Pete! I mean, it's not Squeep! I mean—"

"I'll actually call the police," said Felix. "One more step, and I'll actually call them!"

In the corner of my eye, I saw a large, fast-moving

thing closing in on us. A white football jersey. A blond kid, sprinting, extended a long left arm and swiped Pete the lizard out of Felix's hand.

Felix gazed round-mouthed at his empty palm.

Then, looking up at the runner, he made small wispy sounds of *actually . . . actually . . .*

"That wasn't actually Thor," I said.

Without looking at me, he turned and chased after the football player.

As he ran, Felix pulled a phone from his pocket.

CHAPTER 19

GOSSIP

Had everything gone horribly wrong, or was this all part of some weird plan of Kayla's? I was leaning heavily toward "horribly wrong."

As I hurried down the central stairs to meet her outside my music class, the bell rang.

The hallways crowded with kids changing classes, kids talking, laughing, arguing, goofing around, blissfully oblivious of what was about to happen—of what I had already *seen* happen.

I felt jealous of them. How unfair that I had to know about the black hole and they didn't.

"Did you hear about the horse?" I overheard a girl telling a friend.

A few feet later another one said something about a horse.

Then a third kid mentioned one.

Apparently, there was some juicy piece of horse-related gossip going around. I marveled at the frivolity of their lives. Talking about horses at a time like this.

I stopped halfway down the hall from the music room and scanned the crowd for Kayla. She had said to meet her outside the door, but I kept my distance. I didn't feel up to talking to anyone I knew right now besides her.

Why had she said it was so important that I go to my music class?

I found myself picturing the piano in the Doorganizer. It sat on a pile of other stuff Alice had surely stolen from the music room. I puzzled over the bizarre links and correspondences between the normal outer world and that warped interior place built of secrecy and greed.

"Hey you," said a girl, swatting my arm.

Willow Johansen stepped in front of me.

"I need to talk to you."

"Uh-huh," I said, looking over her shoulder for Kayla.

"You can't be Nev Everly's lab partner," said Willow.

"What? Why not?"

"Are you *kidding*?" said Willow. "You and Nev Everly? Oh yeah, right. Get over yourself, Hap. She is so out of your league."

"What are you talking about?" I said.

"You can be Paisley's lab partner," said Willow. "She was already Lacy's, but Lacy's agreed to be Nev's partner, so you can be Paisley's."

"Huh?" I said. "No way! I'm Nev's partner."

"Well, you're not going to the dance with her," said Willow.

"What dance?" I said.

"Homecoming, dummy," said Willow.

"We're past homecoming," I said. "And sixth graders can't go to the dances anyway. They're for seventh and eighth only."

"I mean next year's homecoming," said Willow. "You have to go with Paisley."

"Paisley hates me!" I said.

"Oh yeah?" said Willow. "Well, she's crying right now about you and Nev and her webbed toe."

"What webbed toe?" I said.

"Paisley's!" said Willow. "She has a webbed toe on her right foot. And you're the only other kid in our class with an abnormality. No one's going to ask Paisley to the dance if you don't."

"Abnormality?" I said.

"Come on, Hap," she said. "Do you honestly think that anyone besides Paisley would *ever* go out with you?"

This conversation had me wondering if a black hole wiping us all out would be such a bad thing.

"And now she's crying," said Willow. "I hope you're happy."

"I didn't even do anything," I said.

"Johansen!" yelled a grown-up voice. "Willow Johansen!"

Ms. Prince, our science teacher, scowled as she strode toward us.

"I am not happy, Willow," said Ms. Prince. "I gave you special permission if you promised to act responsibly. Do you call this acting responsibly?"

"What did I do?" said Willow, staring up at her.

"Remember your science project?" said Ms. Prince. "Did you leave part of it behind in my classroom? Something important, maybe?"

"What?" said Willow.

Ms. Prince reached into the pocket of her cardigan sweater, pulled out a lizard, and held it under Willow's face.

"Look," she said, "I'm not going to let you and Felix continue with this project if you can't eve—"

The word froze on her lips the moment I grabbed the lizard out of her hand.

I stumbled backward with Squeep!

Willow and Ms. Prince stared wide-eyed, both of their mouths falling open.

Turning, I heard their screams start up like police sirens, drawing every pair of eyes in the hallway toward me as I ran in the wrong direction from the music room.

CHAPTER 20

THE YELLOW BACKPACK

Barreling around the corner, I nearly collided with the security guard known as Santa Claus. Recognition dawned in his eyes as he looked from my face down to Squeep!

He lunged for me as I passed him, his big white wedding-banded hand missing my ear by inches.

Now I heard him chasing me. His shoes slapping, huffing and puffing, dangerously close and getting closer.

I thought, *Shouldn't I be faster than this old guy?*

But Santa proved to be one tough senior citizen.

He dove at me, his head slamming into my lower back hard enough to knock me off my feet and send Squeep! soaring out of my hands.

Ascending toward ceiling tiles, Squeep! stared down at me flying below him. He winced as I plowed into a crowd of students, knocking at least five of them over. As I fell through a collapsing tackle of bodies, I tried to keep my eyes aimed at where Squeep!, reaching the top of his arc, began to fall. His body rotated counterclockwise as it descended into the waiting hands of Kayla.

She caught him with a gentle lowering motion, while I slammed hard into the floor, a rockslide of bony kids coming down on top of me.

My eyes fought to stay open against somebody's kicking shoe.

Kayla placed Squeep! into her yellow backpack and zipped it mostly closed. Holding the bag by its top strap, she headed off down the hallway and turned right at the first corner.

Instantly, from that direction, a deep, adult voice shouted her name.

"Freeze, Kayla!" it yelled. "Get on the floor with your hands behind you!"

Kayla's yellow bag came back into view, sliding across the floor to stop about twelve yards from where I lay under the crush of kids.

Then Kayla herself followed, stumbling backward away from a large running man in an FBI windbreaker. His hand thrust down for her wrist.

Kayla reversed directions with a twisting dive. The man looked surprised as he plunged headlong over her to the floor, his gangly legs whipping his shoes into the lockers in a thumping crash.

Before Kayla had rolled to her feet, two more FBI guys

fell upon her. As she slipped through one's legs, the pair of men tangled and tipped.

But now Kayla had four new running agents surrounding her. Now five. Now six. I saw the flash of panic in her eyes as, dodging one agent's hand, she came within the grasp of two others.

Then three of them had hold of her at once, forcing her arms behind her back. A small agent in a suit leaped in with a pair of flashing metal handcuffs.

Kayla howled the word "NO!" as Detective Frank Segar cuffed her wrists together behind her back.

"Get her secured in a vehicle," Frank yelled at the blond FBI woman lifting Kayla into the air. "I want her clamped down."

As the female agent carried her away, Kayla stared down at the yellow backpack. Then her eyes crossed the floor to where I lay, before her face disappeared around the corner.

"Clear these hallways!" yelled Frank, reaching for the walkie-talkie on his belt. "This is an emergency lockdown, people! Get everyone into the rooms. No one comes in or out while we're on lockdown."

"Mobile one, mobile one, this is team leader," Frank said into his walkie-talkie. "Kayla Conklin is in custody. Beth Conklin remains at large. I repeat, the subject remains at large. Use extreme caution. Radio team leader before you engage . . . Hey you, security! Get these kids into the rooms!"

"Okay, you heard him, everybody . . . ," Santa Claus started saying.

As kids got up, I turned my face toward the floor. Frank hadn't spotted me yet, and I sure didn't want him to. I could see his shiny black size-four FBI shoes standing beside Kayla's backpack, where something stirred below the yellow canvas.

"Officers," yelled a familiar voice. "Actually, Officers!"

Felix walked through the formation of agents, waving his hands in the air.

"Officers, I'm actually the one who phoned the police," said Felix. "I am the victim here. It was my property that was stolen. And the thief is actually lying on the ground right there!"

Felix pointed at me. I turned my face back to the floor.

"He actually had one known accomplice," said Felix. "Number fourteen from the varsity football team, last known whereabouts—"

"Shut up!" yelled Frank. "And get into a classroom, before I kick you into one!"

Frank began stepping toward me.

"Actually, Officer . . . ?" said Felix.

As Frank's shoes approached, a flickering in the distance shifted my focus to the farthest end of the hallway.

I saw four galloping horse legs. Now I heard their hoofs beating.

I looked up in time to see a flash of the full animal before it passed from view.

Had I gotten knocked in the head too hard?

No. The FBI agents saw it too and were yelling:

"There she goes, sir!"

"Six o'clock, sir! There she is! Six o'clock!"

"Go! Go! Go!"

The whole flock of black FBI shoes alighted at once as the agents raced down the corridor in the direction of the horse.

Felix chased after them, flapping his arms and yelling, "Officers! Actually, Officers!"

I started moving toward the yellow backpack, slithering at first, still afraid of being spotted, my left leg aflame with pain. I pulled myself up and started to crawl, slowly at first, then accelerating.

I skittered like a lizard across the floor.

As I reached out for the backpack, a hand swung down and yanked it away into the air.

I locked eyes for an instant with Dimitrius, before he turned and ran off with Kayla's bag.

CHAPTER 21

THE SWITCH

Limping as fast as I could hobble, I chased Dimitrius's number 07 jersey down the same hallway where once, after our first encounter, I had pursued him with his own wallet. This time he left me even farther in the dust.

He turned right, toward the gym, and I found myself alone in a corridor that felt creepily empty after the chaos behind me.

A loud banging sounded up ahead.

It came from within the shop room. Something violent clanged against the inside of its big steel door, like a trapped animal fighting to get out.

Limping past, I looked in through the narrow window of safety glass at the infuriated face of the blond FBI woman who had carried Kayla away.

She hammered her fist against the locked door.

Seeing me, she started yelling swear words.

I turned and kept on limping down the hallway.

Around the next right, I saw Dimitrius sprawled out on the ground clutching his stomach. He had had the wind knocked out of him.

I scanned the floor for the backpack. When I didn't see it, I followed his gaze farther down the corridor.

Twenty yards off, I spotted Kayla, her hands still cuffed behind her back. She staggered along like a drunk in a movie.

Rushing toward her, I saw that she carried her backpack in her mouth by its top strap.

"Kayla," I said, running, breathless. "Kayla, wait!"

She turned toward me, revealing a nasty scrape across her forehead. She had a dizzy, dopey, extremely un-Kayla-like look in her eyes.

"What happened?" I said.

"Ah habba fa ma heb," she said.

I took the backpack out of her mouth.

"I had to fall on my head," she said.

She looked near fainting.

"Come here," I said, guiding her toward an empty classroom. "We need to get out of the hallway."

I glanced back at Dimitrius. He lay watching us from the floor with his cell phone in his hand.

I shut the door behind us.

"Tell me this is all part of your plan," I said.

"I don't remember," she said, wincing. "I'm so dizzy I think I might throw up."

"Great," I said, unzipping her backpack. "Well, plan or not, we've got to do this right now."

I took out Squeep!

"Hey there, buddy," I said. "It's time to boogie."

"No, not here!" yelled Kayla. "You have to be in your music class, or else nothing will line up right."

"What does that mean, 'line up right'?"

"You have to be in the place where . . ." Kayla trailed off.

A look of pure terror came over her face.

"Oh no!" she said, pointing. "That's not Squeep!"

"What?" I said. "Of course it is."

I looked down at the lizard, who kept flicking his tongue out around his upper mouth, searching for the missing mustache.

"That's Pete!" said Kayla. She looked ready to burst into tears. "Oh no! No! NO!"

"Then where's Squeep!?" I said.

"I think Alice has him," said Kayla. "No, Hap! We can't let her get back inside the Doorganizer! That's the one thing we can't let happen."

"She won't get back in," I said. "She doesn't know how

it works. You have to put Squeep!'s tail into his mouth, and she'll never figure that—"

As I spoke, Kayla leaped toward me as though to block the words before they came out of my mouth.

But she was too late. She turned and stared into the empty classroom.

I followed her eyes up to the PA system on the wall.

"Alice can't hear us through that thing, can she?" I said.

It clicked and erupted with blaring, mocking sound:

"*'Alice can't hear us through that thing, can she?'* Wah-ha-ha-ha!" laughed the amplified voice of Alice. "HA-AHAHA! *'Alice can't hear us through that thing, can she?'* . . . Oh, thank you so much, Hap! You're right, I never would have figured it out on my own. I've got your little friend Squeep! right here, and he wasn't being any help at all, were you, Squeep!?"

My mind flashed back to Dimitrius lying in the hallway with his phone in his hand. He must have been telling her which room we entered.

"Ha-ha, were you, Squeep!? Were you, Squeep!? HA-HA-HA!"

Alice fell into hysterics, her laughter zigzagging across the line between joy and madness.

CHAPTER 22

WHEN SISTERS FIGHT

"**N**o, Alice!" I yelled. "You don't understand! You have to believe us. We're—"

Kayla nudged me with the elbow of one of her hand-cuffed arms.

"Come on," she whispered. "It's time to go."

I was struck by how back-to-normal Kayla suddenly looked. No longer dizzy or panicked, she seemed, if anything, relieved.

I stared at her as we jogged back into the hallway.

"I can't answer that yet," said Kayla.

"Did you mean for that to just happen?" I yelled, then realized she was back to evading my questions before I even asked them.

I recalled her words about Alice from earlier: *When she's like this, the only way to tell her the truth is to lie to her, and the only way to lie to her is to tell her the truth.*

130

Now Kayla took a running leap into the air. Swinging her chained wrists under her feet like a jump rope, she landed with her hands cuffed in front of her instead of behind.

"Give me Pete and my backpack," she said.

I passed her the lizard and bag.

Kayla put the one inside the other, then handed me back the nacho chip I had given her that morning—as though this were a perfectly logical transaction.

"Now hurry to your music class," she said. "Don't ask any more questions or we'll run out of time."

As she said the word "time," I heard a distant *fuhp!*

Something whished by between Kayla and me. It impaled itself into the wall next to the extinguisher.

I stared in disbelief at . . . an arrow.

Like an archer's arrow. Like a time-flies-like-an arrow.

Kayla walked toward it.

"Did that just fly out of my mind?" I said.

"No, not your mind," said Kayla as she pulled the red metal fire extinguisher off of the wall. "Beth's."

But I had already spotted her, coming around the corner out of the gym.

Atop the largest horse I had ever seen in my life sat an ancient Mongolian warrior. He pulled another arrow from a quiver on his back.

"That's Genghis Khan," I said. "Is Beth Genghis Khan?"

Fuhp! The arrow flew from the bow straight at me.

Kayla swung the fire extinguisher outward by its black hose.

Swat-clang!

"Yes," said Kayla, knocking it away. "Now run to your music class before she kills us."

As I backed away down the hall, Genghis Khan fired three more.

Fuhp! Fuhp! Fuhp!

Kayla fell forward, swinging the red tank out in front of her. As it ricocheted between the first two arrows, deflecting them, Kayla landed on her knees with her arms high above her head. The third arrow sparked fire as it broke the chain between her handcuffs.

Genghis Khan scowled.

Kayla rushed toward him, spinning the fire extinguisher.

Spurring his horse to charge, he fired arrow after arrow after arrow.

Fuhp! Fuhp! Fuhp! Fuhp! Fuhp! Fuhp!

I turned and ran away as fast as I could, feeling that faint queasiness I always got in the pit of my stomach when my sisters were fighting.

As I rushed down the corridor toward my music class, the hallway clock read 11:03.

Why would Kayla want Alice to get back into the Doorganizer?

If she thought Alice could stop the black hole, she was sadly mistaken.

What could Alice do against those giant crystal monsters? What could Kayla do for that matter? Squeep! hadn't been able to stop them. That's why he kept asking *me* for help.

Me!

I was the one they were hunting. So only I had even a chance of stopping them.

But how could I get back inside without Squeep!?

I looked down at the nacho in my hand.

Oh, how I hated riddles!

What did the nacho mean?

CHAPTER 23

MUSIC CLASS

Tardiness to Mr. Stanley's music class was never an issue.

Nobody even noticed me as I walked in.

As usual, Stan the Man sat at the teacher's desk rocking out to his headphones—probably something he had recorded himself the night before on his keyboard and bass guitar.

Meanwhile, the students wandered around experiencing what he called "free-form learning" with the musical instruments. Though at least half the kids usually just sat and talked.

Today, entering that loud chaotic room felt like returning to the scene of the crime. There they all were, everyone who had first fallen into the Doorganizer: Nev Everly, Dana Mosley, Jake Harrison, Doug Melman, Davina Tyler, Stan the Man . . . Everyone exactly where they were when it had happened. Or, rather, when it *would* happen, any minute now.

I looked up at the clock, which had somehow jumped past 11:05.

I felt the angularity of the nacho in my fingers.

I needed to *act*. But I couldn't even think.

I realized that for a while now, I'd been silently praying.

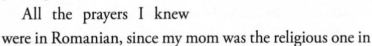

All the prayers I knew were in Romanian, since my mom was the religious one in our family. I didn't get what half the words meant, but I went on saying them. I had a feeling they might help.

As I approached Nev, she tapped the empty desk beside her.

I sat down.

"Are you busted?" she said.

"Huh?"

"They called you down to the office," she said. "So did you get busted for something?"

"No."

"Are you okay, Happy?" she said. "You look a little wiped."

I nodded.

"Hey, can I tell you something?" she said. "I don't want to be rude or forward or anything, but there's an opinion I need to share. Or else it's gonna drive me crazy."

"Okay," I said.

"That," she said, pointing at my face, "would be the exact right length for your beard. Except a few of the hairs seem to grow faster than the other ones. If you just trimmed those, it would look amazing."

Rolling my eyes slightly, I looked away from her.

"Sorry," she said. "I'm being rude, huh?"

"No, it's fine," I said. "You're actually the first person to ever like my beard at all. So I guess that's something that had to happen at least once before the world could end."

She laughed, and the weirdness of her laugh made me smile despite myself.

I got an idea.

"Nev," I said. "You're good at riddles. You figured out the Easter Island thing right away."

"Well, that was easy," she said.

"Can you help me solve another one?" I said.

"Okay," she said, smiling, "but on one condition."

"What?"

She reached into her handbag and took out a small pair of scissors.

"If you let me trim your beard in, like, one or two places," she said.

"Fine," I said. "Can you trim and think at the same time?"

"Of course," she said, leaning in close.

She started snipping at my face with the scissors.

"Okay," I said. "Here's the clue. This nacho chip. It means something. Like it represents something else in the world besides a nacho. The same way the egg and quarter did."

Nev paused in her snipping to look down at the nacho for a moment.

"Well, that one's even easier," she said, going back to snipping.

"What?" I said. "What does it mean?"

"That's me," she said, snipping. "That nacho means me."

"You?" I said. "How does it mean you?"

"Look," she said.

Taking the chip from my hand, she turned it counter-clockwise, so the broken end was on the bottom. Suddenly, I saw what she meant.

It was shaped like Nevada.

"Nevada . . ." She pointed from the chip to herself. "Nevada. See?"

"Yeah," I said.

Going back to work with the scissors, she said, "So whatever little scavenger hunt you're on, if that chip is the question, then I'm the answer."

Nevada, I thought. The poker chip had had the words "Las Vegas." Las Vegas, Nevada. Had Squeep! meant the Doorganizer was in the state of Nevada?

No, he must have meant . . .

Nev leaned back to survey her work.

"Fantastico," she said. "This looks so good, Happy, you're not even going to believe it."

She reached into her purse and pulled out a makeup compact in the shape of a seashell. She held the mirror up to my face.

"See?" she said. "Check yourself out."

My mouth fell open.

"Huh," she said. "I didn't think it was that shocking."

"Where did you get that compact?" I said.

"At the thrift store," she said. "Pretty cool, huh? I think it's real silver. The flaw is that someone replaced the original mirror with one that's too thick. So it doesn't close all the way."

She shut the compact, but the glass stopped it from fastening.

"The old mirror's still behind this one," I said, taking it from her hand.

"Huh?" she said. "Then why would they put a new one in?"

"To keep it open," I said. "And to protect you from looking inside."

"What?"

"Nev, something really weird's about to happen," I said. "I have to break this mirror."

"Yeah, right," she said.

"Then I'm going to vanish," I said.

"You're going to *vanish*," she said.

"Yeah," I said. "Like disappear before your eyes."

"No," she said. "You can't disappear now. I just got you looking halfway decent."

"When it happens, don't start screaming," I said. "You can't freak out too badly."

"I'm freaking out a little already," she said.

"Good," I said. "Better you freak out now. Because after it happens, you have to do something *very important*."

"What?" she said.

"Close the compact, and don't look inside," I said. "Do NOT look inside. Just close it. Will you be able to do that?"

"Of course," she said. "But you're messing with me, right?"

"Okay," I said. "I think you're going to do it. Good. Now I gotta go. Please don't tell anyone about this."

Lifting the compact high, I slammed its mirror down on the desk as hard as I could.

A thick *crack!* Nev jumped a little, her eyes wide with fear.

A couple kids not busy playing instruments looked back at us.

I didn't want to vanish with them watching, so I waited one last moment for their eyes to drift away.

I lifted the compact from the desk. At the same time, Nev clamped her hand down over mine.

"This is happening, isn't it?" she said. "You're really about to go somewhere."

"Yeah, right now," I said.

"For how long?" she said. "An hour? A day? A week?"

"I don't know," I said.

"But not forever, right?" she said. "You're going to come back?"

"I don't know," I said.

She pressed down on my hand harder.

"Tell me you're going to come back," she said. "Or I won't let you go."

"I'm going to come back," I said.

"Okay," she said, lifting her hand from mine. "Now you better really vanish. Or I'm going to feel so stupid."

"Don't worry," I said, tipping the compact up toward my eyes.

I felt that old, unnerving seamlessness as I slipped back inside.

I stood exactly where Squeep! had brought me earlier, in the same flashing darkness, at the same spot on the junk pile.

The only difference was that this time I knew what to do.

Glancing back at where I had come in from, I watched the shell-shaped portal to the music room close like an eye and disappear.

Thanks, Nev, I thought.

Walking toward the gigantic crystal monster, I held my hands high in the air.

I started shouting the words before the long beam of its spotlight eye reached me.

"I surrender!" I yelled over and over again. "I'm Happy Conklin, and I surrender!"

PART 3

CAPTIVITY

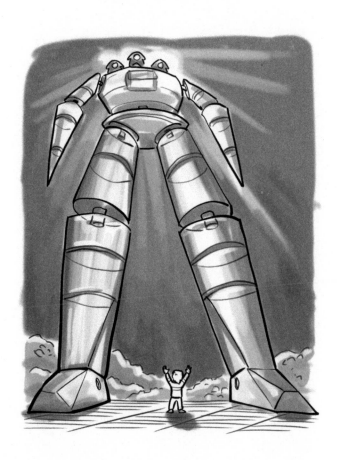

CHAPTER 24

THE OUROBOROS

I kept my eyes on the creature's arms, those enormous crystal shards with spiked tips that I knew could puncture the Doorganizer and obliterate the Earth.

"I surrender!" I kept yelling.

The owl-head beamed its bright light down upon me.

"Take me," I said, wincing. "I'll go! But leave Earth alone!"

Other spotlights glided closer, revealing themselves to be projected from flying creatures—two more cyclops owls, like the "head" of the crystal giant.

As they flew, their beams rolled toward me across the junk-strewn floor. The closer one illuminated another person in the Doorganizer, only about ten yards away: my sister Alice.

She hid behind a pile of stuff, staring at me in terror and holding Squeep!, who must have brought her here.

The big creature either hadn't noticed her or didn't care she was there.

I brought a finger to my lips to say *keep quiet.*

She nodded.

Squeep! stared at me from her hands.

What happens now? I thought.

Squeep! held up a green kazoo.

What's that supposed to mean?

A loud *shunk!* overhead interrupted my thoughts.

Looking up, I saw that the two flying creatures had removed a transparent cylinder from the giant's chest.

They swooped this cylinder down upon me, trapping me inside and then scooping me up like a bug in a jar.

I tumbled to the bottom of the container, my face smooshing against the thick glass. Alice stared up at me.

Squeep! lifted the kazoo as I rose into the air.

What had the kazoo meant?

The drones carried the cylinder up the creature's enor-mous chest and, slid-ing it back into its slot, trapped me in a crystalline prison.

The ground shifted beneath me like an earthquake as the colossus began to walk, with loud crunching footfalls, toward the portal to the deep-blue world.

The good news was that the monster was leaving with-out destroying the Earth. The bad news: it was taking me with it.

The colossus climbed through the circle, out of the Doorganizer, and into the blueness on the other side.

As we passed through, I saw that the reverse side of the circular portal had been formed by an enormous curving silver ring, carved in a pattern of reptilian scales that reminded me of something . . .

Grandma's ring.

The portal looked like a giant circular serpent biting its own tail. The Ouroboros, but with a face more lizardy than snakelike. It looked a little like Squeep!'s face.

As I marveled up at it, one of its huge eyeballs rolled down at me.

It was alive! A living Ouroboros the size of a freight train.

It opened its huge jaw, releasing its tail from its mouth. Instantly, the portal to the Doorganizer vanished.

The Ouroboros uncoiled upon the air. It had six legs, black irises, and a long fluid body covered in scaly silver mail.

Its head and Squeep!-like eyes fixed down upon me while, all around us, its body twirled like the tail of a kite.

Meanwhile, the two owls had detached and were

lowering my glass cell down toward a transport barge that floated in midair.

Upon this barge, monstrous man-size creatures fastened my cell to its platform.

My captors were all hideous to look at.

This one in the black hooded cloak, whose face resembled a giant insect's body, was by far the worst:

After my first glimpse at him, I clutched a hand to my chest in fear I was having a heart attack. That's when I found, in my shirt pocket, a folded piece of paper that hadn't been there earlier.

I knew it was a note from Kayla before I unfolded it. She must have slipped it into my pocket back at school without me noticing.

CHAPTER 25

KAYLA'S NOTE

Dear Happy,

If you're reading this, it means you stopped the black hole and we're all still alive. Thank you! It was the only possible way, but I couldn't tell you that without making the decision for you.

And it wasn't my decision to make.

I knew that if I let you come to it on your own, you would do the right thing.

If there had been ANY other possible way . . . or if I could have gone in your place, I would not have hesitated.

I'm already working to help you get home.

It's not going to be easy. We will need Alice's help. That's why I got her back into the Doorganizer. She had to watch you do what you—hopefully—did with her own eyes. Otherwise, in her current mental state, she wouldn't have believed me about the threat or that you surrendered yourself to save the planet—and her precious closet—from destruction.

Now we can count her as an ally. And we're going to need her and the power of the Doorganizer to get you back.

Please try to keep yourself safe and alive until I can figure out how to get to you.

Love,
Kayla

P.S. Sorry this wasn't one of my usual notes. I wish I could see into the Doorganizer, but I can't, so I don't know what's happening or what's going to.

I had already guessed that it wasn't one of her usual notes.

Normally, Kayla's notes were all smeared with eraser marks, because Kayla could see the face of the person reading her words in the future. She tended to revise a lot based on different reactions. If you asked a question aloud while reading one of her regular notes, you'd likely find the answer written in the next line.

But Kayla couldn't see into the Doorganizer, so she couldn't see where I was now.

Was she planning to use Alice's help to come through the Doorganizer to rescue me?

Dad had been very worried the last time Kayla had gone in there. He believed that mixing Kayla's powers with those of the Doorganizer could be particularly catastrophic.

But, then again, Dad had believed emphatically that a living creature could not be a portal. And I was staring at proof that he had been wrong about this: the giant Ouroboros, flying along beside my captor's craft, stared at me with its huge Squeep!-like eyes, while its body zipped fluidly around the skyscrapers of the gigantic alien metropolis.

CHAPTER 26

THE IMPERIAL PLANET

I journeyed in my glass prison across a planetscape both wondrous and terrifying—though mostly terrifying.

The last alien world I visited had been cloaked in an unending nightmare of darkness. This one, at least by first comparison, looked like a bright, magnificent dream.

Its sky arched wider, bluer, and more brilliantly than our own.

The transport drifted like a bug through a forest of dazzling skyscrapers. Sculpted of gemlike materials, each one stood taller than any on Earth. Vertical gardens grew upon them like moss over tree trunks.

At first, I dared not look down from so high an altitude.

When I finally worked up the nerve, I saw the surrounding buildings drop toward a single, misty vanishing point—not even a glimpse of the ground.

My prison cylinder stood on a long hovering craft, guarded by military-police types. I avoided looking at my captors' hideous faces. Instead, I concentrated on the scenery.

We passed fountains larger than Earth's skyscrapers, floating spherical gardens, and wide pedestrian promenades where crowds began to form.

It might have been the most beautiful experience of my life, if not for the gathering mobs of monsters who wanted to kill me.

Every face in the multitude screamed hatred and murder.

I tried to tell myself that, since I was new to this culture, maybe their expressions and body language didn't mean what I thought they meant. For all I knew, this was their way of giving a stranger a nice welcome.

As though to clear up any such confusion, the mob raised signs and banners with colorful drawings of me getting my head cut off and my guts ripped out. Others held up giant Happy Conklin Jr. effigies, which they then lit on fire and beat with sticks.

As sickening as this was to behold, I had to admit that these beings were pretty talented artists. Truly excellent paintings and sculptures can impress you even if you don't necessarily agree with the point they're making. And as draftsmen and artisans, these guys were simply phenomenal. I bet any one of them could have gotten hired at Disney.

Realizing that this technologically advanced, culturally sophisticated, diverse, and cosmopolitan civilization unanimously wanted me dead almost gave me a heart attack.

So I looked at the Ouroboros swimming eel-like through the skyscrapers. Its eyes looked so much friendlier than everyone else's.

Do you know Squeep!? I thought, staring back.

It drifted closer.

Squeep! sometimes seemed capable of reading my mind. Maybe the Ouroboros could too?

Hey you, I thought as though it could hear me, *I'm good*

friends with a reptile. An Earth lizard named Squeep! Do you know him? . . . He knows how to do that same trick where he becomes a portal by biting his tail . . . Did you teach him that?

It drifted closer and closer to our flying craft.

Can you help me? I thought. *Please? Squeep! would want you to help me. We're best friends . . .*

The Ouroboros lifted its frontmost right arm.

It held something tiny in its enormous flipper. I squinted at the tiny speck. It was a kazoo! A green kazoo just like the one Squeep! had held up, only a whole lot bigger.

My captors grew angry at the creature for flying so close. They started screeching and bellowing and threatening it with their weapons.

The Ouroboros turned away, like a rope through a pulley. It zigzagged off into the sky, where it faded into the blue brilliance.

Now my captors screeched and bellowed at me.

I couldn't understand any of the barbaric garbling, but I knew threats when I heard them.

I tried to make the monsters less scary by giving them nicknames based on my favorite kinds of candy.

So this guy became "Gummy Bear."

I named this one Nutrageous.

Unfortunately, the nicknaming trick didn't work on the scariest of the creatures, the one standing across the deck from my cube staring coldly into the depths of my soul:

This guy so horrified me that thinking of him as "Jelly Belly" or "Twizzler" or "Jolly Rancher" only made it worse.

Though I didn't know it yet, I had every reason to fear this individual above all others.

He was Star Chamberlain, Lord High Torturer of the entire Empire. He controlled a vast, finely tuned network of secret police, informants, torturers, prisons, dungeons, thugs, and murderers reaching across the hundred thousand planets of the Empire like a nervous system of fear and pain.

Luckily for the health of my pounding heart, I didn't know any of this yet. Nor did I know that the black, castle-like skyscraper now swallowing our craft was his headquarters, the Ministry of Agreement.

As we docked, the hatch of my glass cell popped open, and I found I could still breathe.

Gummy Bear and Nutrageous pulled me out of my seat, manacled my wrists, shackled my ankles, and then chained the manacles to the shackles.

They confiscated my backpack and everything in my pockets, including Kayla's note, which I guess I probably should have eaten or something.

Then Gummy Bear and Nutrageous marshaled me down an enormous white corridor.

After several minutes, we stopped, and Nutrageous pressed his clawed paw against the wall. A previously invisible door *whooshed* open, and they led me into a big white room.

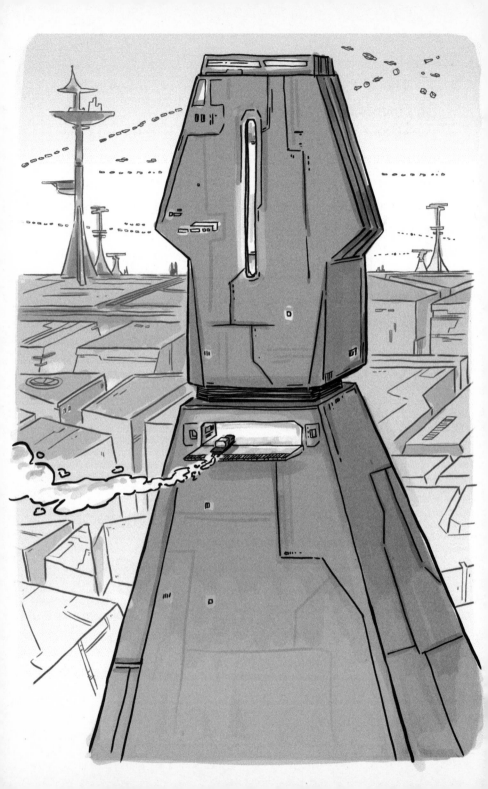

There stood the largest creature I had encountered since the gigantic crystal monster who had carried me out of the Doorganizer.

But this one, I recognized.

It felt good to see a familiar face—even his.

"Gubbins!" I said.

"Ack. Hello, Happy Conklin," said Ack Gubbins.

CHAPTER 27

THE PROTOCOL

Whooshing shut, the door vanished so completely into whiteness that I lost track of its location until Gummy Bear posted himself beside it.

Nutrageous unlocked and removed my chains. I figured he was the turnkey, responsible for doors and restraints, and Gummy was the muscle, in case I got out of line.

Ack smiled down at me, though I could tell he wasn't happy.

His species had skin that changed colors involuntarily to reflect their innermost feelings, making them some of the worst liars in the universe. I knew from my time as a Gubbins that gray was the color of fear—the paler the gray, the deeper the terror.

Ack Gubbins looked nearly as white as the room.

"So, Ack," I said. "How's it going?"

"Ack," he replied.

"You said it, buddy. Ack is right."

"Ack, Happy Conklin, ack, I am here to teach you, ack, the Imperial Protocol, ack. Please listen, ack, and . . ."

Though his voice and throat worked strenuously to articulate the human words, I had trouble understanding him.

I pointed to my ear.

"I'm not getting all of that," I said. "And I don't remember how to speak Gubbinsglopf. Why don't you do what we did last time? Mirror my communication by using the Perfect-O-Specs?"

Ack slapped my mouth shut with his lower right hand.

"Ack, do not talk of evil, illegal devices," he said. "Ack. All, ack, Conklin products have been banned, ack, throughout the universe. Ack, speak of them, ack, and you will be killed."

I followed his eyes to Gummy, who had his claws on the hilt of some weapon at his belt.

"Don't mention the products," I said. "Got it."

"Ack, good. Now, ack, you must learn the Imperial, ack, Protocol."

"No!" I said. "I'm not learning any Imperial ack whatever-the-ack, until you tell me what's going on! Why'd they bring me here? Am I under arrest? What are the charges? Who's my lawyer? And it better not be you!"

Ack grew so scared that patches of his white skin flickered into transparency, revealing flashes of his innards that I still wish I'd never seen.

"Oh gross," I said.

"Ack, Happy Conklin, ack," he said. "You will soon be in the, ack, presence of the Emperor. You must not, ack, make any mistake of Imperial Protocol, ack. Or else . . . ACK!"

Ack made a cutting motion below his neck.

"They'll cut my head off?" I said.

"No, ack," he said. "*My* head."

"What?" I said. "Wait, so if I mess up my curtsy or whatever to the Emperor, they'll cut *your* head off?"

"Ack, yes," he said. "Also please, please, please, ack, don't curtsy, Happy Conklin."

"Well, no wonder you're so pale," I said. "Okay, what's the stupid protocol?"

Ack breathed a sigh of relief that turned him from translucent and white back to a pale gray.

I spent the next several hours memorizing every rule, sound, gesture, and action that Ack felt I might need to know to keep him alive.

The hardest move to master was called the Sublime Genuflection. Everyone had to do it the moment the Emperor or any member of his family entered the room. First you fell to your knees, then onto your face, then you made this half-gargling, half-yodeling noise until the Emperor grunted.

UGALUGALUGALUGA...

UGALUGALUGALUGA...

My first attempt at the gargle-yodel sounded so awful that Ack turned transparent again.

But as I practiced, his skin grew opaque and gradually less pale.

I could tell I had gotten good at it when I saw faint patches of orange appear on his belly.

Once he felt confident that I had learned the Sublime Genuflection, he began going over all the other rules.

I learned you must never look directly at the Emperor's face or those of his family members. Also, never take a step in the Emperor's direction, unless he instructs you to with a particular grunt and hand gesture. Then, you have to avert your eyes and make a full Sublime Genuflection between *every single step* you take as you approach him.

169

Every step? I thought. *How did these weirdos ever manage to build an empire in the first place?*

Soon Nutrageous returned with the manacles, shackles, and chains.

As he locked me up like Houdini, I thought about Squeep!, and wondered what he had been expecting me to do about all of this.

"Ack, please, Happy Conklin!" Ack cried weakly as they led me out. "Please, ack, remember to, ack . . ."

"I'll do my best," I said, before the door *whooshed* shut.

CHAPTER 28

IN THE DOCK

They marched me back down the white corridor, which I now realized was composed of opaque cells like the one I had left.

We halted at the threshold of a different sort of room, crowded with important-looking creatures in fancy garments.

It struck me as a cross between a royal court and a judicial one.

On the far right, an empty throne decked out in fancy regalia stood upon a raised altar. On the left side, at the front of the courtroom, an insectile, bug-eyed judge presided over things from a high desk.

At first, those assembled in the gallery seemed like refined, distinguished, aristocratic types. But the moment they saw me, they became as loud and unruly as the mob outside.

They jeered, howled, stomped, and banged on tables as guards marshaled me toward the bug-eyed judge, who barked at the crowd to come to order, presumably.

Gummy Bear led me to the dock, a rectangular enclosure to the lower right of the judge's bench. Without undoing any of my restraints, Gummy stepped behind me to my right.

Glancing back, I saw his claws on the hilt of the weapon at his belt.

As I started to wonder whether I'd be able to do a proper Sublime Genuflection in my manacles and shackles, a hornlike instrument blared several notes. Everyone in the room fell first to their knees, then onto their faces.

I did my best, despite the chains and restraints. What my Sublime Genuflection lacked in form, I more than made up for with my spirited yodel-gargling, which I thought was as good as anyone's.

After an exhausting minute or so of this, the Emperor grunted, and we all rose back to our feet or foot-like appendages.

Though I never looked toward him, I couldn't help getting some sense of the Emperor's appearance out of the corner of my eye.

The Emperor was surprisingly small—maybe only a few inches taller than me. He was about fifty percent head, and his head was about forty percent nose. Unlike the statues of his ancestors on Easter Island, he was orange-colored.

After the bug-eyed judge's opening remarks, a long thin creature stood up from a desk. He or she looked like a giant walking stick in a suit.

After bowing low toward the throne, Walking Stick began to stroll about the room and yammer.

Without understanding a word, I recognized Walking Stick right away as the district attorney type, a skilled politician with relatable body language and a manner of studied persuasiveness.

He or she directed everyone's attention to a holographic orb in the center of the room as the lights began to dim.

The footage must have come from a camera attached

to one of the cycloptic owls from the Doorganizer—a bird's-eye view of me running across the junk pile yelling, "I surrender! I surrender!"

Good, I thought. Evidence of my cooperation should incline the court toward leniency.

Next the orb showed footage from the *Wrastlinsanity* match, where Grandma and I had fought as a tag team against Florida Pete. Walking Stick yammered over close-ups of Grandma and me shaking hands, and then repeated close-ups of us tagging each other during the match.

I realized that Walking Stick was explaining the concept of tag-team partnership to the court. I wanted to yell out: "It's just a wrestling match! It's a game! That doesn't make us partners in real life!"

Luckily for Ack Gubbins, I resisted this urge and kept my mouth shut.

Now the orb cut to higher-definition holographic footage from some outdoor event on the Imperial Planet.

A multitude of spectators lined floating boulevards for a parade honoring the Emperor. The camera drifted along over spectacular floats, marching bands, kicklines, streamer-dancers, acrobats—the works.

The Emperor and Empress watched from atop a high colorful pyramid. As the camera moved closer, I saw the pyramid was more of a ziggurat formed of carpeted stairways leading up from street level.

Upon the flat triangle of its apex, the Emperor and

Empress sat on crystal thrones while beautiful alien ser-
vants attended to their every whim.

The royal couple smiled slightly and looked down at
the festivities.

Then their eyes popped open in surprise as a lightning
bolt from above struck carpet only yards away from them.

At first it seemed like a magic trick, perhaps part of the
spectacle, as a figure leaped up from the lightning's black
scorch mark.

But this creature wasn't part of the parade.

It was Grandma, running toward the Emperor.

She wore her spangly flamenco catsuit. Her head was
bare, her face fully visible to all as she lifted the Emperor
out of his throne.

Hoisting him over her head, she body-slammed him to the carpet.

She kicked her leg high in front of her as she elbow-dropped onto the Emperor's midsection.

An enormous gasp came up from the crowd.

As I wondered where his bodyguards were, the camera cut to many of them running up the steps from places around the ziggurat.

Now it cut back to Grandma slapping her hand forward and backward across the Emperor's wobbling nose. The beautiful alien guards were no help. They had all fallen on their faces and were yodeling.

But now the Empress attacked, leaping from her throne and swinging a crystal goblet.

Grandma caught her by the arm, took hold of her skirts, and swung the Empress around in circles as though giving a child an "airplane ride."

When Grandma let go, the Empress took a fast bounce and went rolling down the stairs like a log.

The Emperor charged furiously at Grandma.

Catching the peak of his head in one hand, she held him back where his swinging arms were too short to reach her.

Her other hand reached in and clutched the opening in his fancy robe. She pulled hard, spinning him out of it completely.

The dizzy Emperor found himself naked except for a pair of frilly underpants, which Grandma promptly yanked down around his ankles.

The Emperor screamed and tried to cover himself.

Either this footage was partly censored or the Emperor's private parts looked like a grid of blurry squares.

As he reached down to pull up his underpants, Grandma kicked him in the butt.

He leaped forward, clutching his rear and howling.

When he bent back down for his underpants, Grandma kicked him in the butt again.

This happened so many more times that I would have thought it was a looped piece of footage if not for all the clear variations in the ways that the Emperor bent down for his underpants and the ways that Grandma kicked him in the butt.

Finally, the Imperial Guard reached the top of the steps.

Seeing them, Grandma shoved the Emperor to the ground and made a vertical gesture with her hand.

In a bolt of reverse lightning, she vanished into the sky.

As the hologram faded and lights came back up, everyone in the courtroom was wailing and moaning over what they had just seen.

They beat their heads with their fists. Several rent their garments and poured ashes on their faces. I had only ever heard about *that* happening in Romanian Bible stories.

I felt that I should be showing outward signs of disapproval too. But all I could think to do was shake my head and frown sternly.

This only served to remind everyone of my presence. They started screaming and growling and chirping at me again, ignoring the bug-eyed judge's calls for order.

Something wet struck me in the head—a splatting, aromatic substance that I could only hope was someone's uneaten lunch.

Something harder hit me in the shoulder.

The judge barked orders at the guards, who lifted me out of the dock and carried me through the howling courtroom.

I shut my eyes as a rain of unknown objects pelted my body.

When I dared open them again, the guards were carrying me down the long white corridor.

Then they *whooshed* open the door of my cell and flung me inside.

CHAPTER 29

BLOOD ROOM

"Oh, ack, thank you, Happy Conklin," said Ack, bright orange with joy. "You kept all the protocols. Ack. Very good, ack. Very good indeed."

"Yeah," I said. "Your head's safe. I wish I could say the same for my own. They're all really mad at me back there. I don't think that the verdict's going to go my way."

"Verdict?" said Ack. "Ack, you're far past the verdict. You were tried in absentia, ack, and found guilty of high treason against, ack, the Galactic Empire. Today, ack, was just your formal sentencing."

"I'm already guilty?" I said. "What's the usual punishment for that? High treason against the Empire?"

"Death, ack, by the most painful means possible," he said. "Ack, of course you'll be interrogated first, ack, tortured, ack, and publicly debased."

"*Oh Doamne*," I said, praying. "Oh God . . . They

can't torture me! What good will it do? I don't know any-thing! I'm an idiot. I have no idea what my grandma's doing or why."

"Even so. Ack. How can they, ack, determine the most painful way for you to die, ack, if they don't explore the possibilities? It's the law."

"*Oh Doamne*," I said.

"Soon, ack, they will come and take you, ack, to the Blood Room. Ack. Thank you again for following the protocol. Ack."

I stumbled away and collapsed beside the white wall.

I was done talking to Ack Gubbins.

I was done saying anything except Romanian prayers.

Before I knew it, Gummy and Nutrageous had returned to collect me.

This time they took me in the other direction down the white hall.

"*Oh Doamne*," I kept saying.

The Blood Room wasn't red like I had expected.

It was muddy black and configured like a hollow pyramid.

The shape seemed to radiate the evil energy of the room's purpose. It looked big enough to accommodate victims far larger than myself.

As they strapped me down onto a table, I realized the murky walls might be covered in blood after all. The dried blood of who knows what kinds of beings, over who knows how many eons.

Now I noticed all the long, rusty instruments hanging on the walls. Huge, heavy, spiked, unspeakable things. Scanning the rows of torture devices, I heard myself scream.

He had been standing there unseen, watching me since I had entered.

Star Chamberlain, the torturer.

One motion from his hand and the guards turned and walked out, closing us into total darkness.

A harsh spotlight came on over my head.

The torturer's face floated in from the gloom.

Upon a horizontal bench, he unrolled a satchel of metal instruments far smaller than those hanging on the wall.

These looked more like tools from a dentist's office.

His long fingers moved through the air above them. He selected one—a green, oddly shaped thing with two large circular transparencies.

Lifting these up, the torturer fitted them onto his own face like a pair of glasses.

I didn't recognize them as Perfect-O-Specs until he flicked the switch.

His misshapen skull re-formed into two buns of white hair.

His horrific jaw became a smile of well-kept human teeth.

Then she stood there, beaming down at me.

"Grandma?"

"Hello, Happy Junior," she said. "Welcome to our new kingdom."

I gasped for air.

"Glad to see me?" she said. "You *should* be. Sorry it has to be in this vile room. For now, it's the only place that we can have any privacy."

"What are you doing, Grandma?" I breathed. "Why did you attack the Emperor? He's going to kill us and destroy the Earth."

"'Attack' him?" she said. "If I had *attacked* him, he'd be a corpse. I merely exposed him. He holds on to power by pretending to be a god. Now that I've shown him for the buffoon he truly is, his reign has started to crumble. So that ours may commence."

"They're going to kill us," I said, "and destroy the Earth."

"Thanks to you," she said, "the Earth is safe, though only for the next few hours. But all the same, nicely done."

"You are so crazy, Grandma," I said. "Disguising yourself? In *this* place, where everyone's after you? How long do you think you can keep that up? I mean, what did you do with the real torturer guy?"

"I killed him," she said. "What? Oh, boo-hoo, poor torturer guy. We are going to make this galaxy a far better place for trillions and trillions of beings, Happy Junior."

"No, *you* are," I said. "Not me. I'm out. Do you hear me, Grandma? I am out!"

"No, partner . . . ," she said.

Reaching, she gently tagged my hand.

"You are IN."